# No Instructions Needed

by Chris "Elio" Eliopoulos

**STONE ARCH BOOKS**
A CAPSTONE IMPRINT

Mr. Puzzle is published by Stone Arch Books,
a Capstone imprint
1710 Roe Crest Drive
North Mankato, Minnesota 56003
www.capstonepub.com

Cataloging-in-Publication Data is available
on the Library of Congress website.

ISBN (library binding): 978-1-4342-6026-0

Ashley C. Andersen Zantop - PUBLISHER
Donald Lemke - EDITOR
Michael Dahl - EDITORIAL DIRECTOR
Brann Garvey - SENIOR DESIGNER
Heather Kindseth - CREATIVE DIRECTOR
Bob Lentz - ART DIRECTOR

Printed in China by Nordica.
0413/CA21300512
032013    007226NORDF13

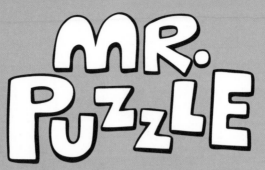

# MR. PUZZLE

## No Instructions Needed

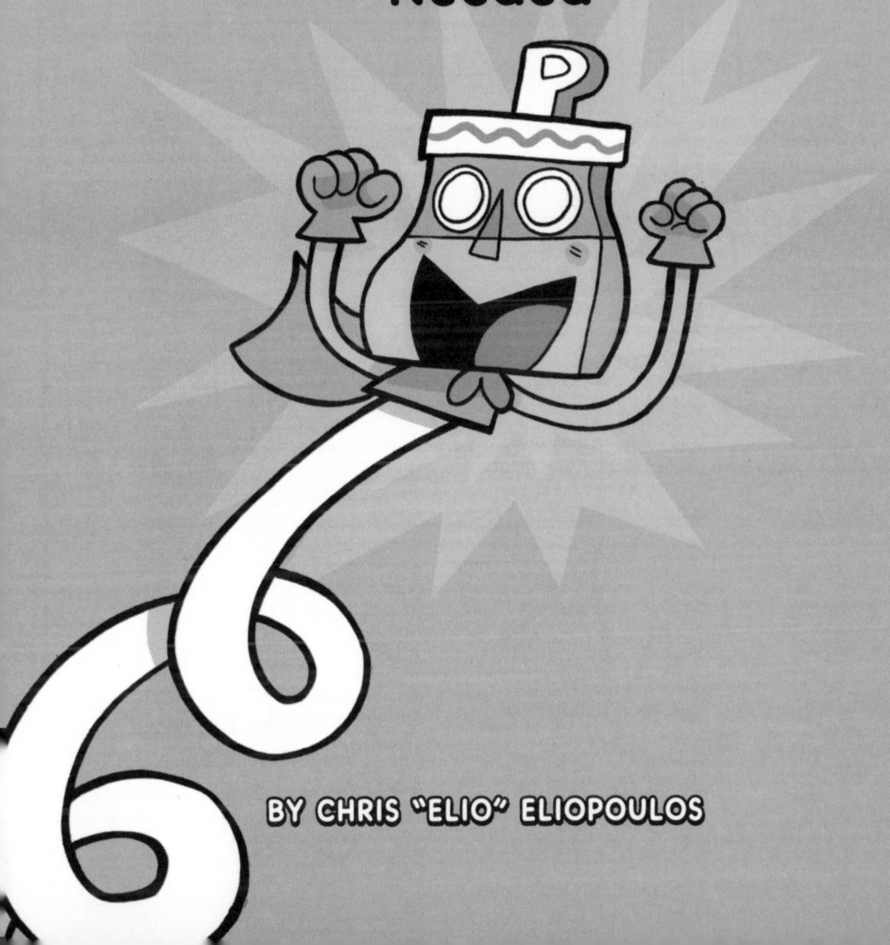

BY CHRIS "ELIO" ELIOPOULOS

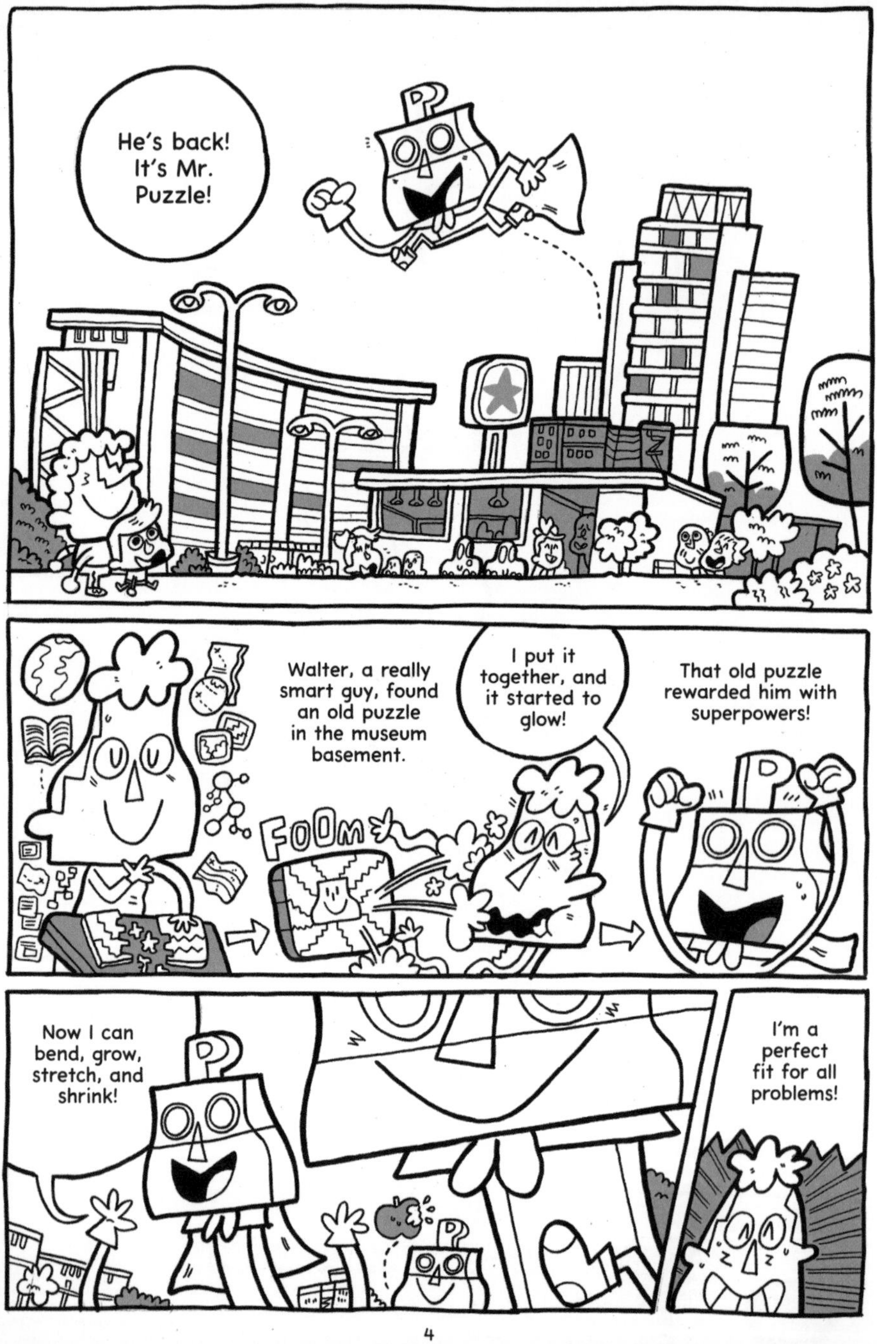
He's back! It's Mr. Puzzle!
Walter, a really smart guy, found an old puzzle in the museum basement.
I put it together, and it started to glow!
FOOM
That old puzzle rewarded him with superpowers!
Now I can bend, grow, stretch, and shrink!
I'm a perfect fit for all problems!

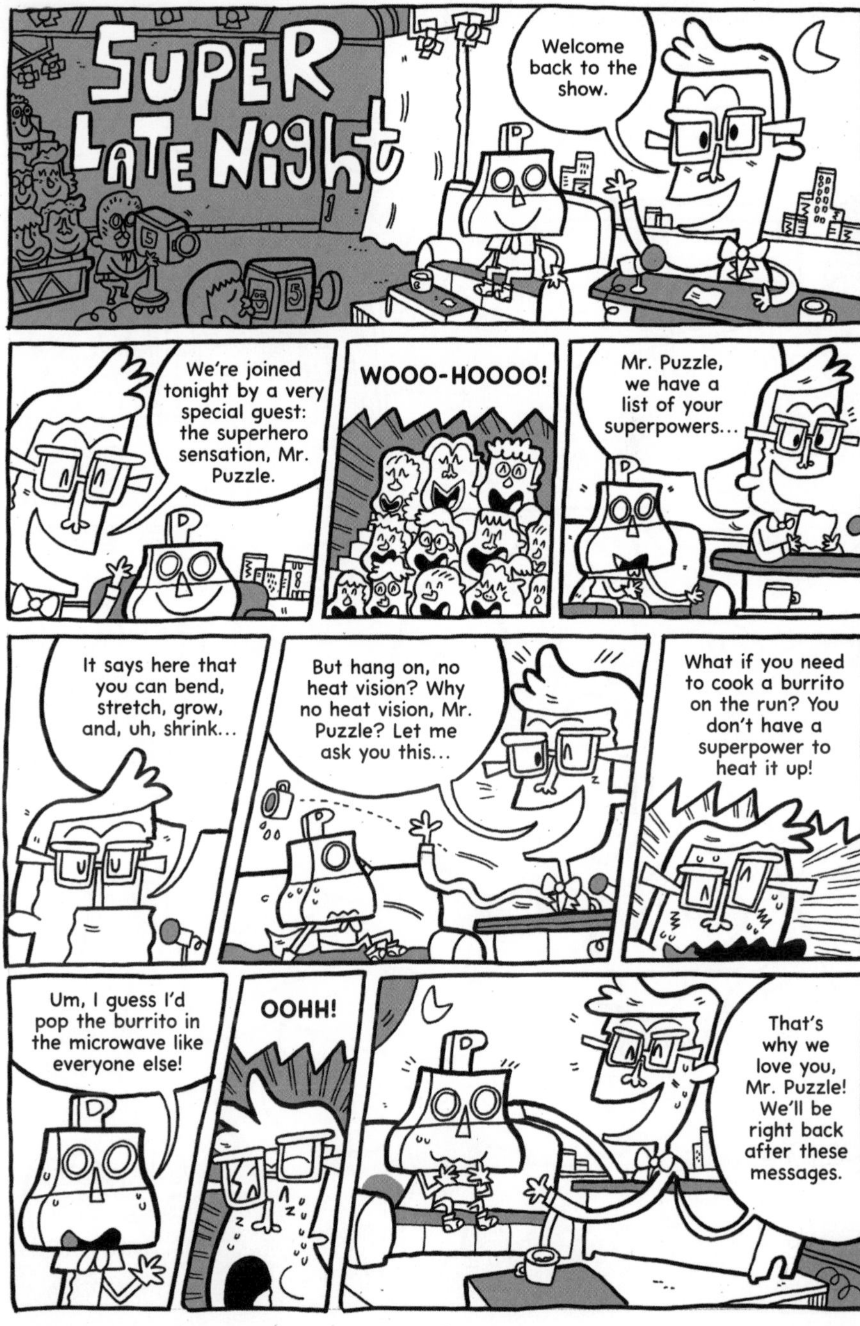
SUPER LATE Night
Welcome back to the show.
We're joined tonight by a very special guest: the superhero sensation, Mr. Puzzle.
WOOO-HOOOO!
Mr. Puzzle, we have a list of your superpowers...
It says here that you can bend, stretch, grow, and, uh, shrink...
But hang on, no heat vision? Why no heat vision, Mr. Puzzle? Let me ask you this...
What if you need to cook a burrito on the run? You don't have a superpower to heat it up!
Um, I guess I'd pop the burrito in the microwave like everyone else!
OOHH!
That's why we love you, Mr. Puzzle! We'll be right back after these messages.

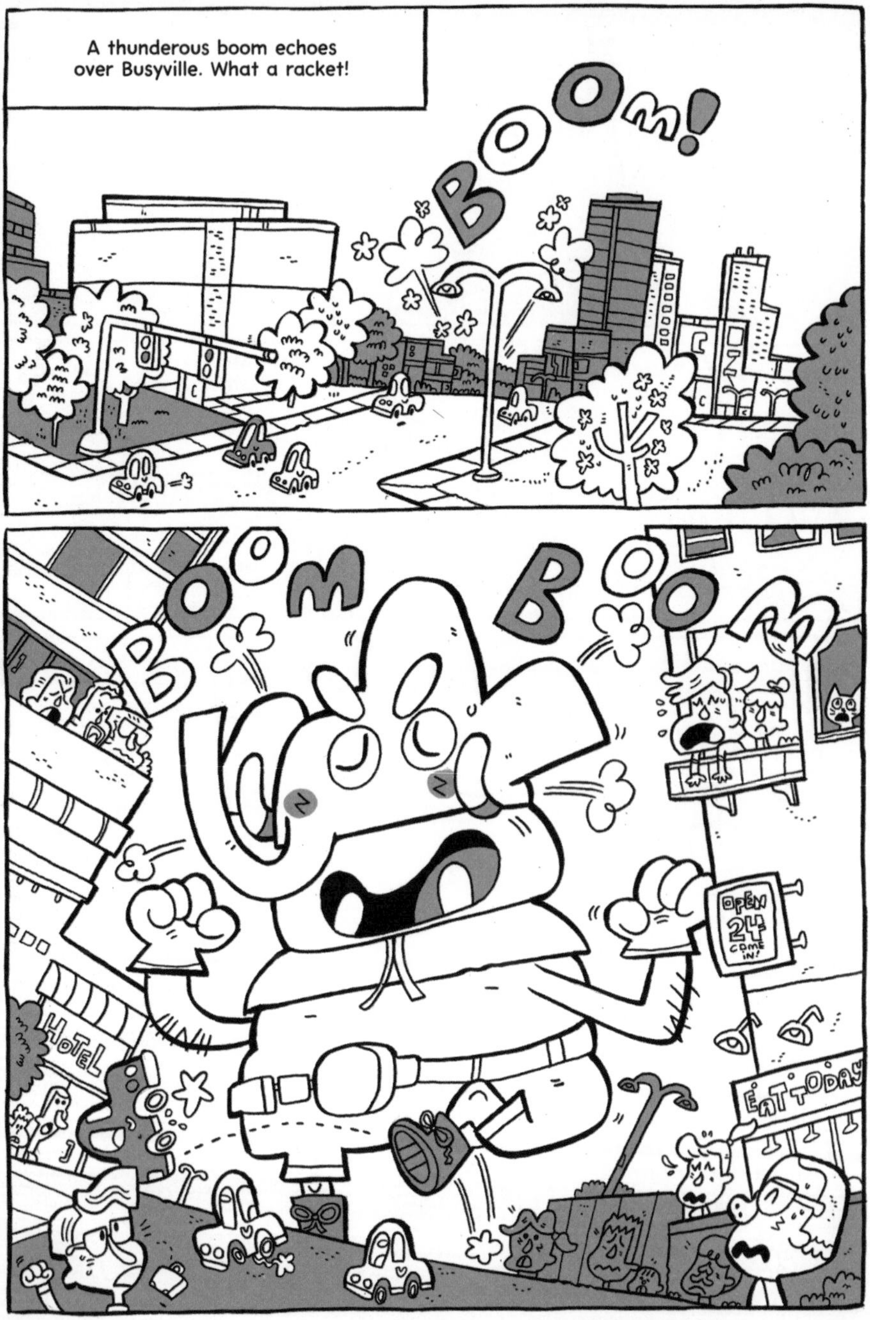
A thunderous boom echoes over Busyville. What a racket!
BOOM!
BOOM BOOM
OPEN 24 COME IN!
HOTEL
EAT TODAY

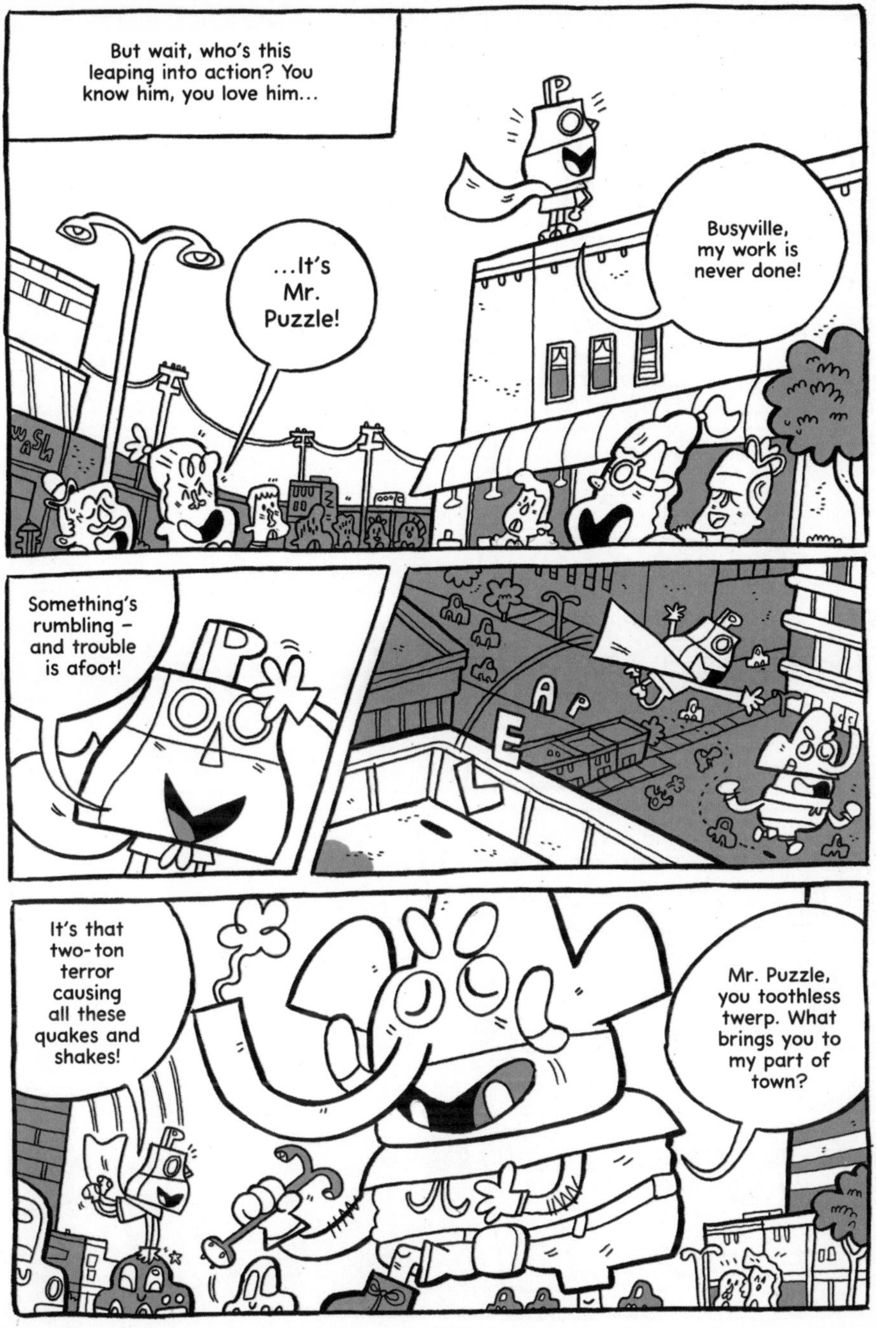
But wait, who's this leaping into action? You know him, you love him...
...It's Mr. Puzzle!
Busyville, my work is never done!
Something's rumbling – and trouble is afoot!
LEAP
It's that two-ton terror causing all these quakes and shakes!
Mr. Puzzle, you toothless twerp. What brings you to my part of town?

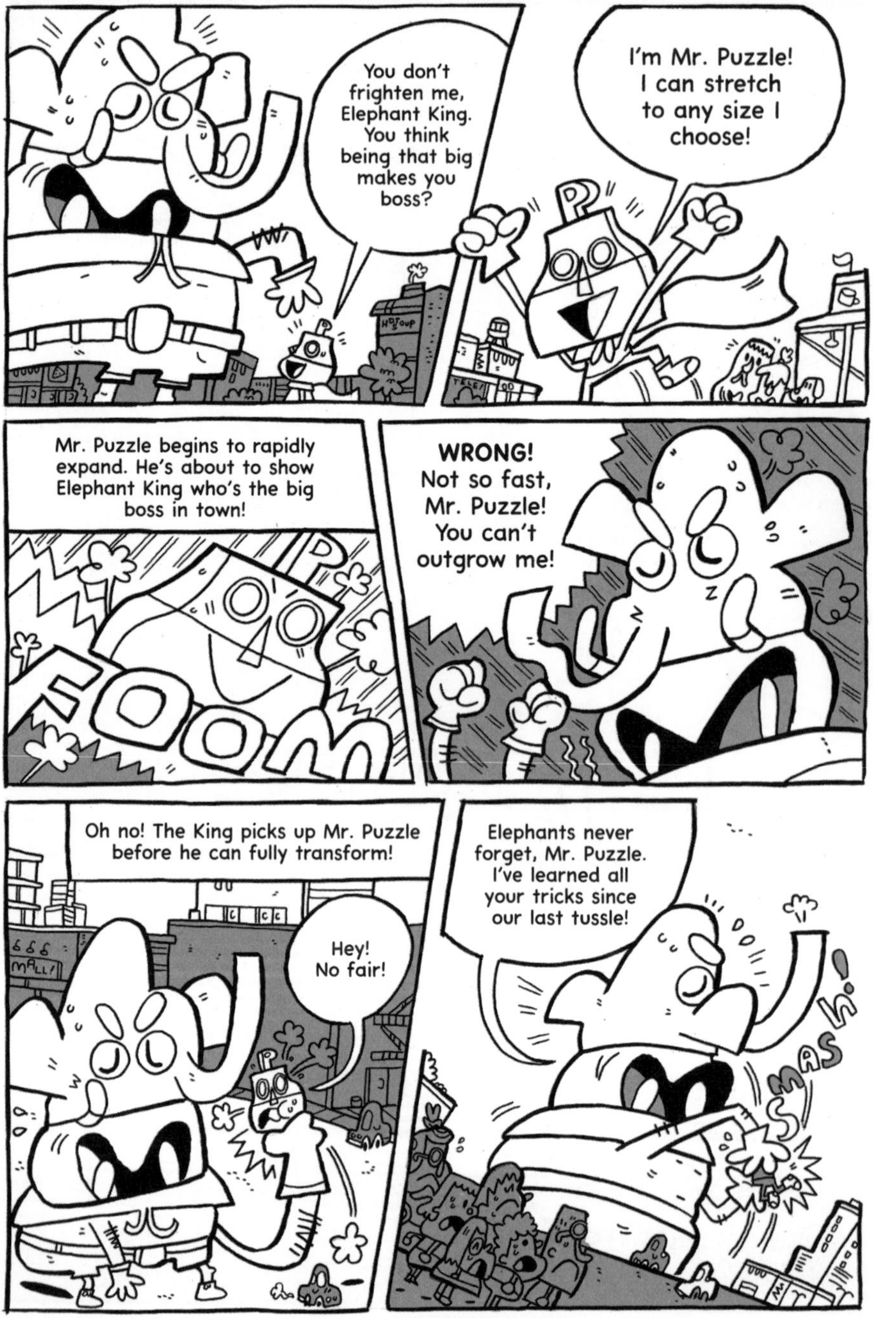
You don't frighten me, Elephant King. You think being that big makes you boss?
I'm Mr. Puzzle! I can stretch to any size I choose!
Mr. Puzzle begins to rapidly expand. He's about to show Elephant King who's the big boss in town!
FOOM
**WRONG!** Not so fast, Mr. Puzzle! You can't outgrow me!
Oh no! The King picks up Mr. Puzzle before he can fully transform!
Hey! No fair!
Elephants never forget, Mr. Puzzle. I've learned all your tricks since our last tussle!
SMASH!

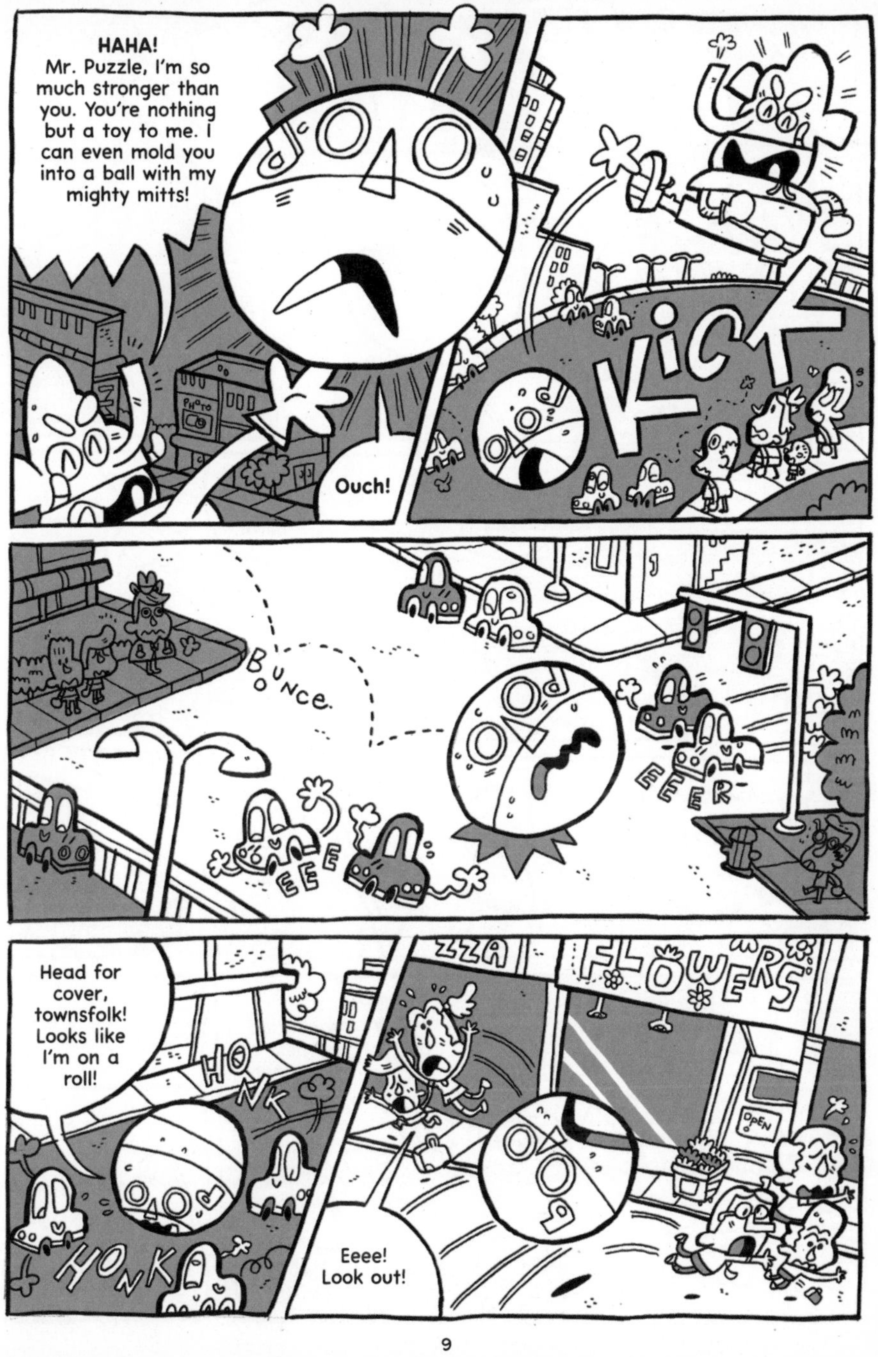
HAHA!
Mr. Puzzle, I'm so much stronger than you. You're nothing but a toy to me. I can even mold you into a ball with my mighty mitts!
PHOTO
Ouch!
KICK
BOUNCE
EEE
Head for cover, townsfolk! Looks like I'm on a roll!
HONK
HONK
ZZA
FLOWERS
OPEN
Eeee! Look out!

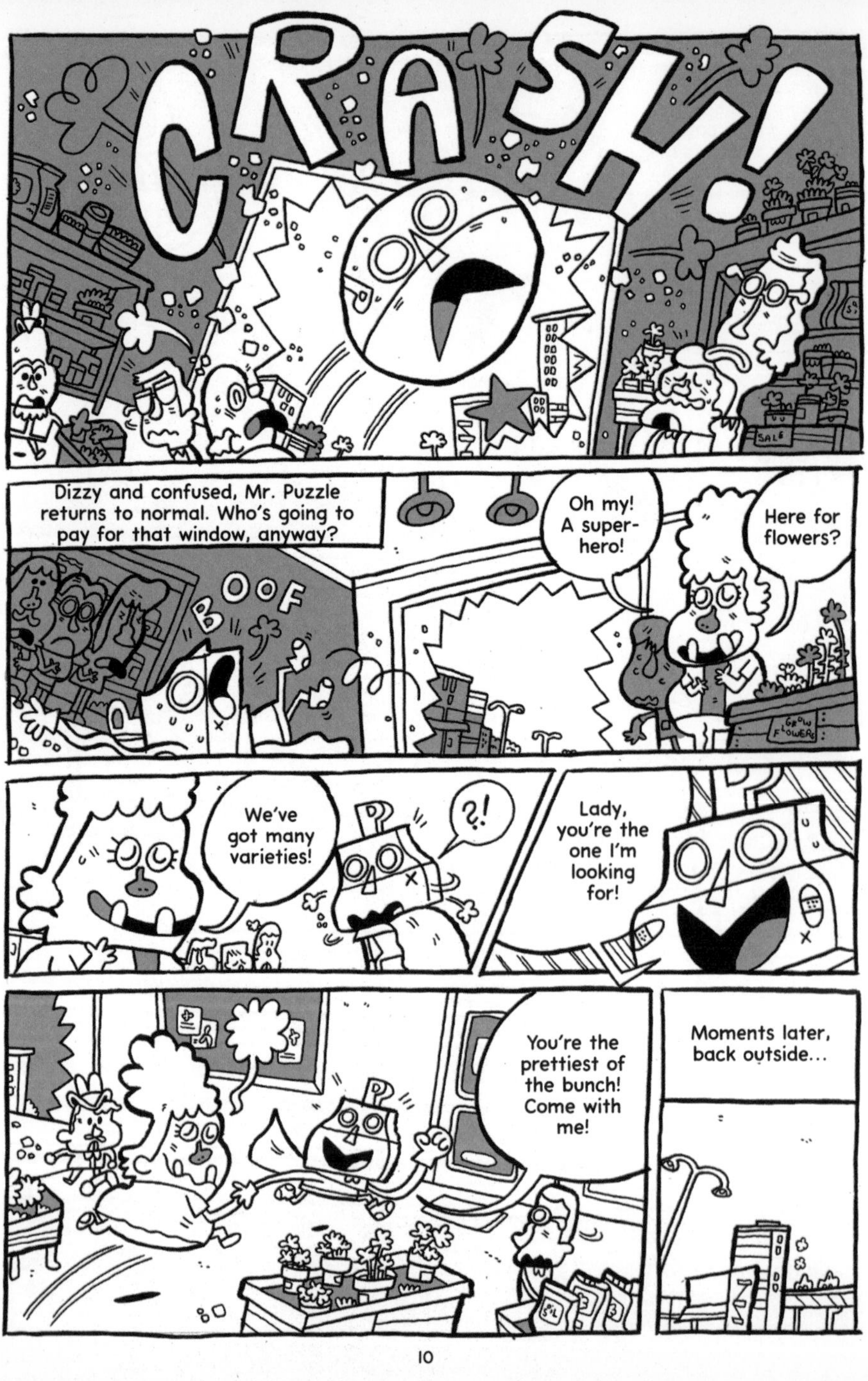

CRASH!
Dizzy and confused, Mr. Puzzle returns to normal. Who's going to pay for that window, anyway?
BOOF
Oh my! A super-hero!
Here for flowers?
GROW FLOWERS
We've got many varieties!
?!
Lady, you're the one I'm looking for!
You're the prettiest of the bunch! Come with me!
Moments later, back outside...

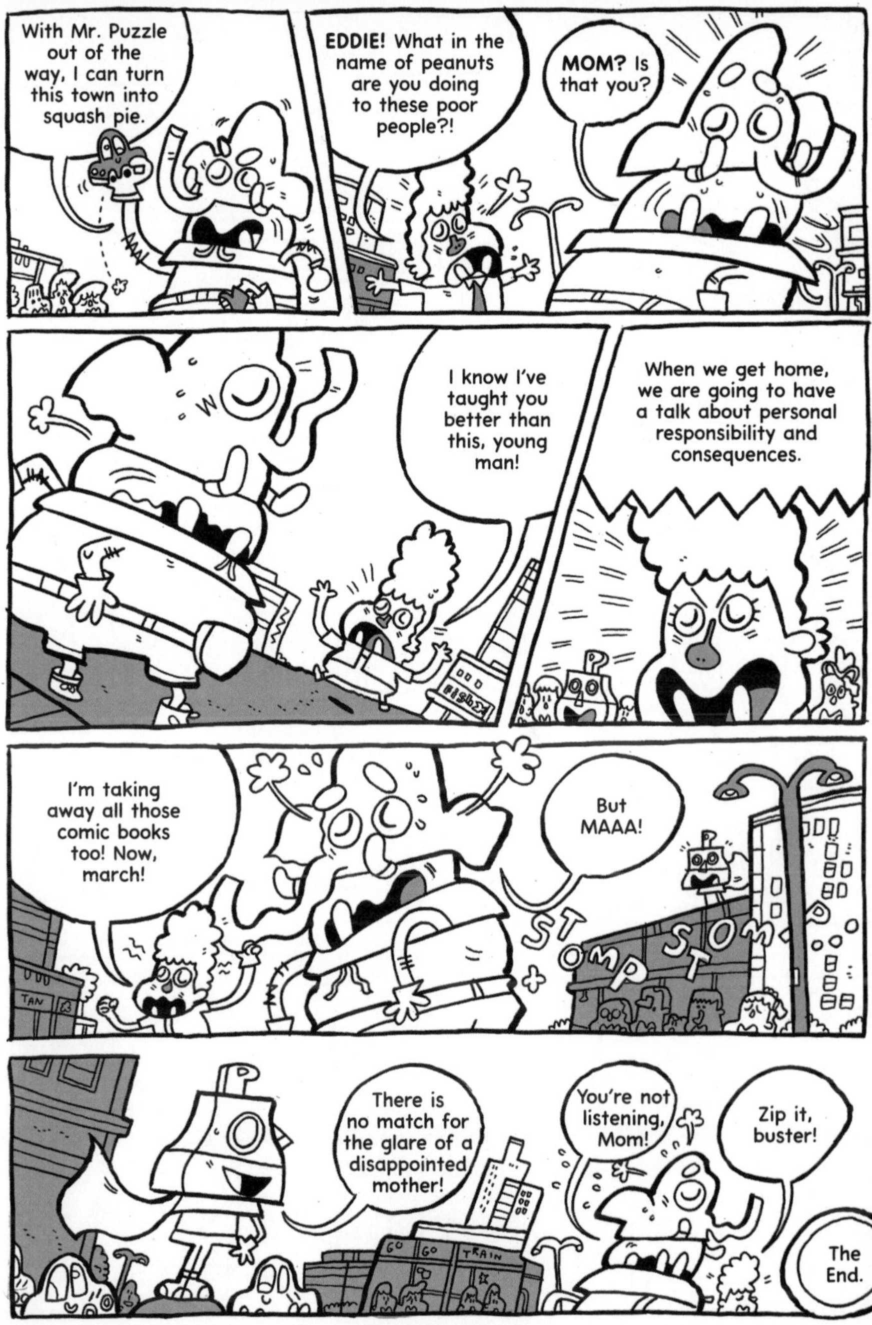
With Mr. Puzzle out of the way, I can turn this town into squash pie.
EDDIE! What in the name of peanuts are you doing to these poor people?!
MOM? Is that you?
I know I've taught you better than this, young man!
When we get home, we are going to have a talk about personal responsibility and consequences.
I'm taking away all those comic books too! Now, march!
But MAAA!
STOMP STOMP STOMP
TAN
There is no match for the glare of a disappointed mother!
You're not listening, Mom!
Zip it, buster!
GO GO TRAIN
The End.

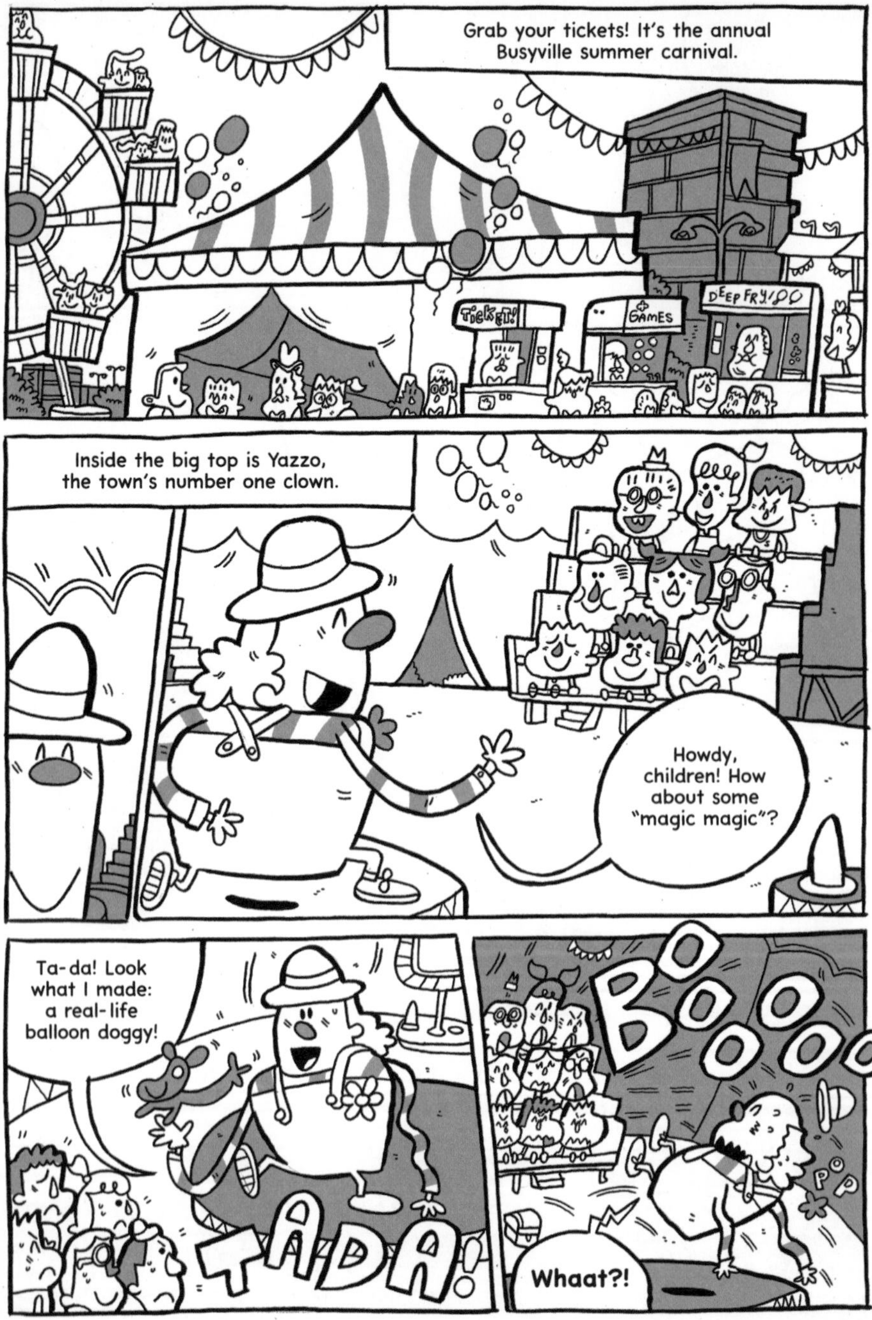
Grab your tickets! It's the annual Busyville summer carnival.
TICKET!
GAMES
DEEP FRY!
Inside the big top is Yazzo, the town's number one clown.
Howdy, children! How about some "magic magic"?
Ta-da! Look what I made: a real-life balloon doggy!
TADA!
BOOOOOO
POP
Whaat?!

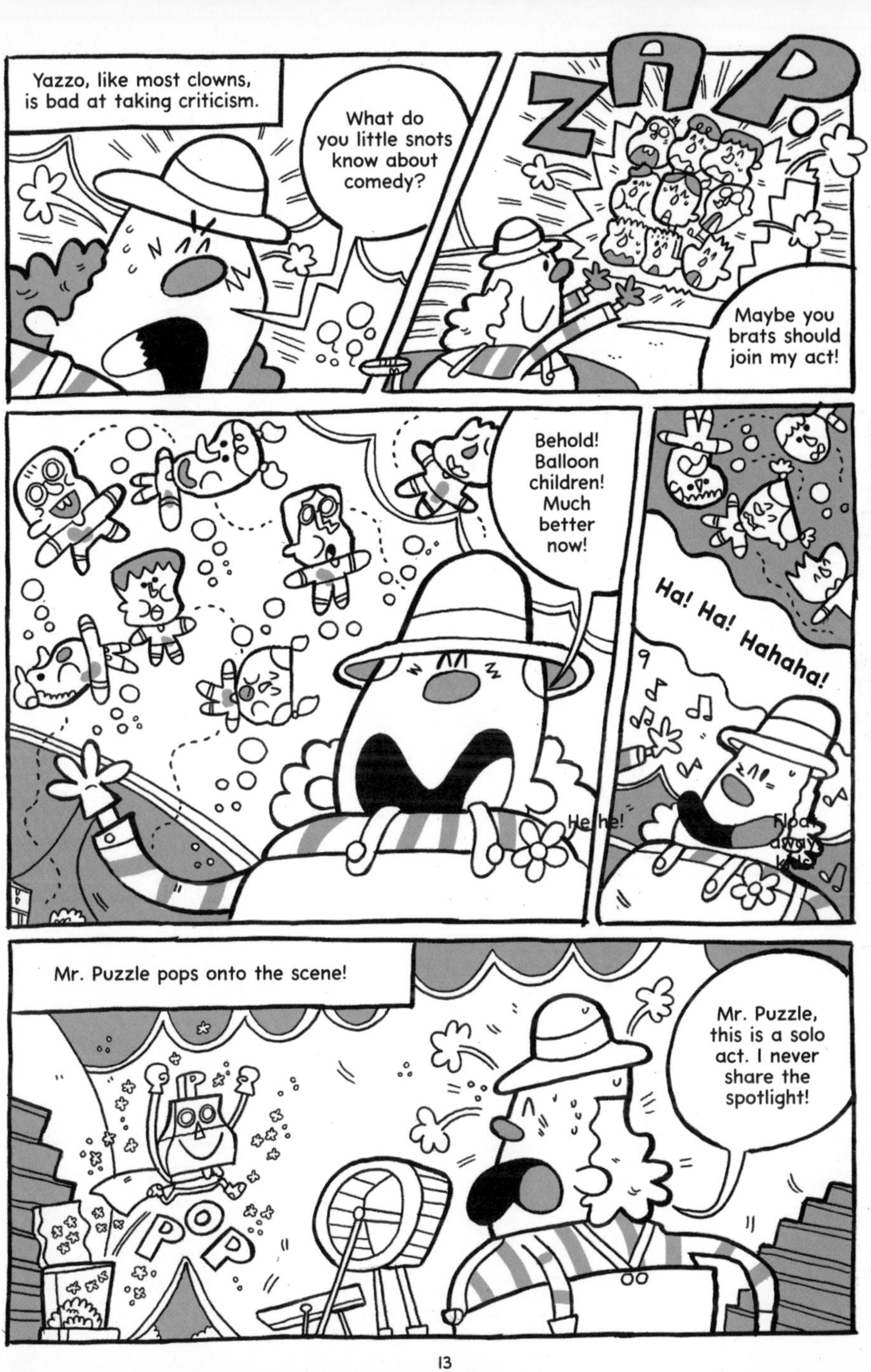
Yazzo, like most clowns, is bad at taking criticism.
What do you little snots know about comedy?
ZAP
Maybe you brats should join my act!
Behold! Balloon children! Much better now!
He he!
Ha! Ha! Hahaha!
Float away, kids!
Mr. Puzzle pops onto the scene!
POP
Mr. Puzzle, this is a solo act. I never share the spotlight!

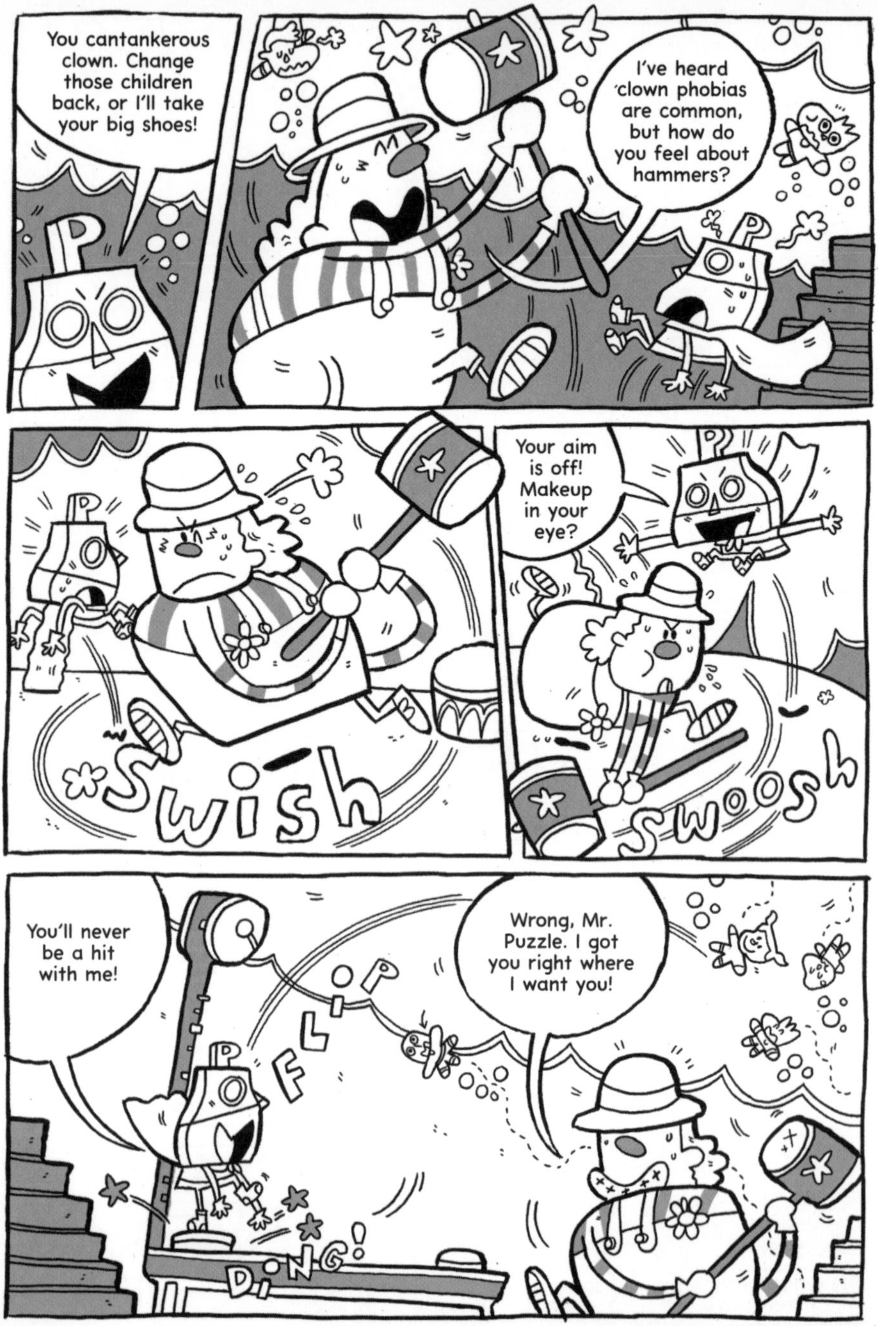
You cantankerous clown. Change those children back, or I'll take your big shoes!
I've heard clown phobias are common, but how do you feel about hammers?
Swish
Your aim is off! Makeup in your eye?
Swoosh
You'll never be a hit with me!
Wrong, Mr. Puzzle. I got you right where I want you!
FLOP
DING!

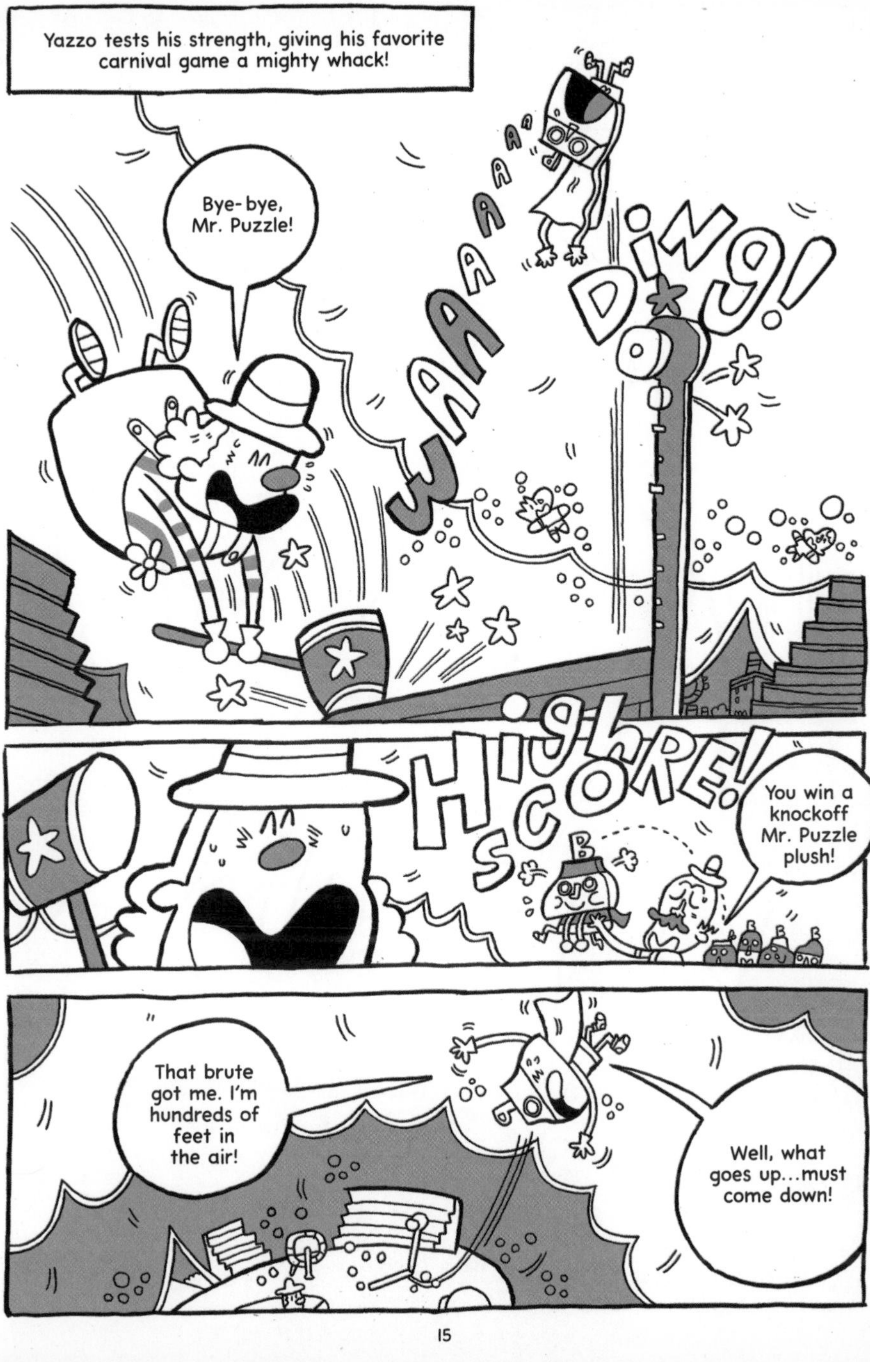
Yazzo tests his strength, giving his favorite carnival game a mighty whack!
Bye-bye, Mr. Puzzle!
DING!
High SCORE!
You win a knockoff Mr. Puzzle plush!
That brute got me. I'm hundreds of feet in the air!
Well, what goes up...must come down!

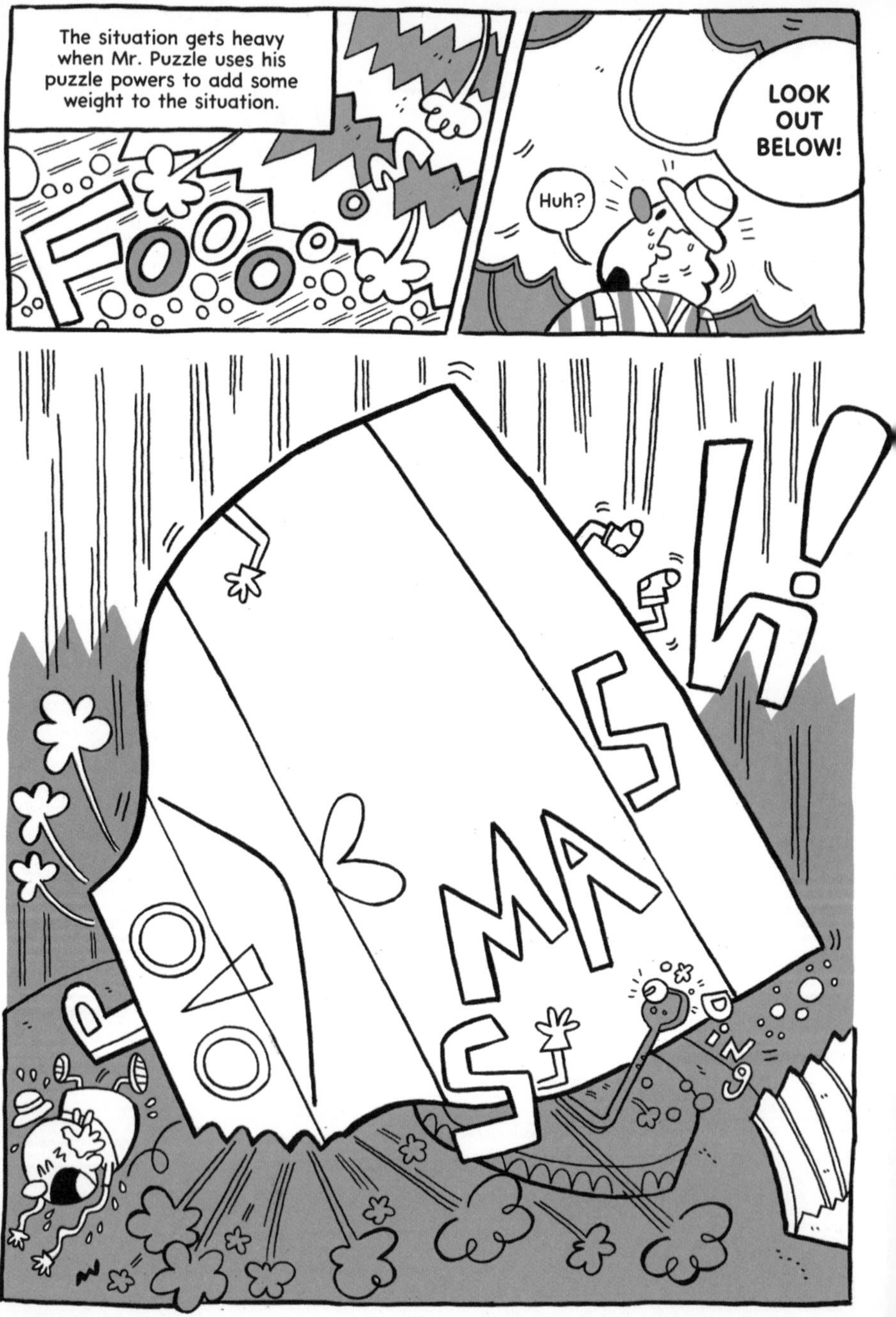
The situation gets heavy when Mr. Puzzle uses his puzzle powers to add some weight to the situation.
FOOO
LOOK OUT BELOW!
Huh?
SMASH!
DING

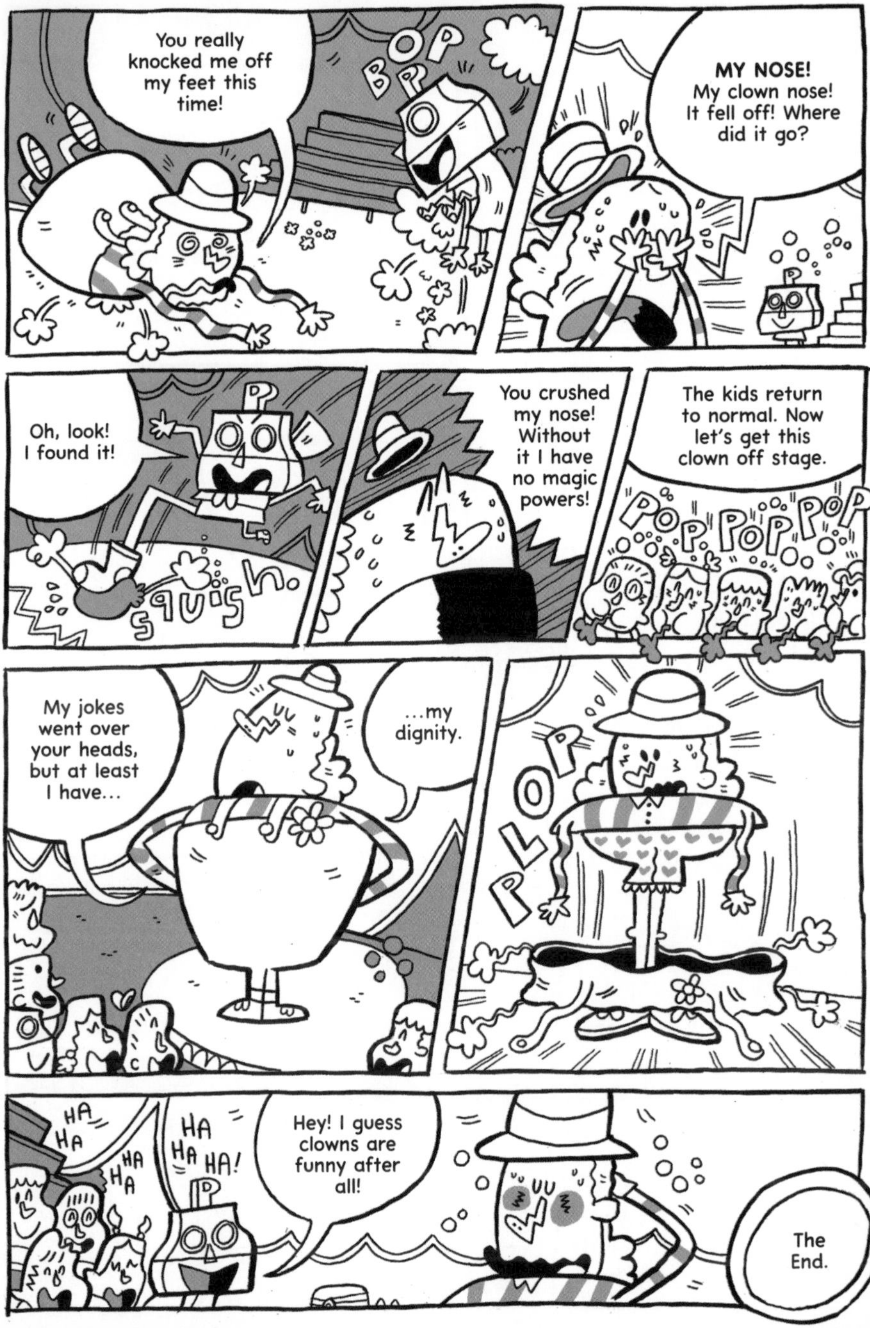

You really knocked me off my feet this time!
BOP
MY NOSE! My clown nose! It fell off! Where did it go?
Oh, look! I found it!
squish.
You crushed my nose! Without it I have no magic powers!
The kids return to normal. Now let's get this clown off stage.
POP POP POP POP
My jokes went over your heads, but at least I have...
...my dignity.
PLOP
HA HA
HA HA
HA HA HA!
Hey! I guess clowns are funny after all!
The End.

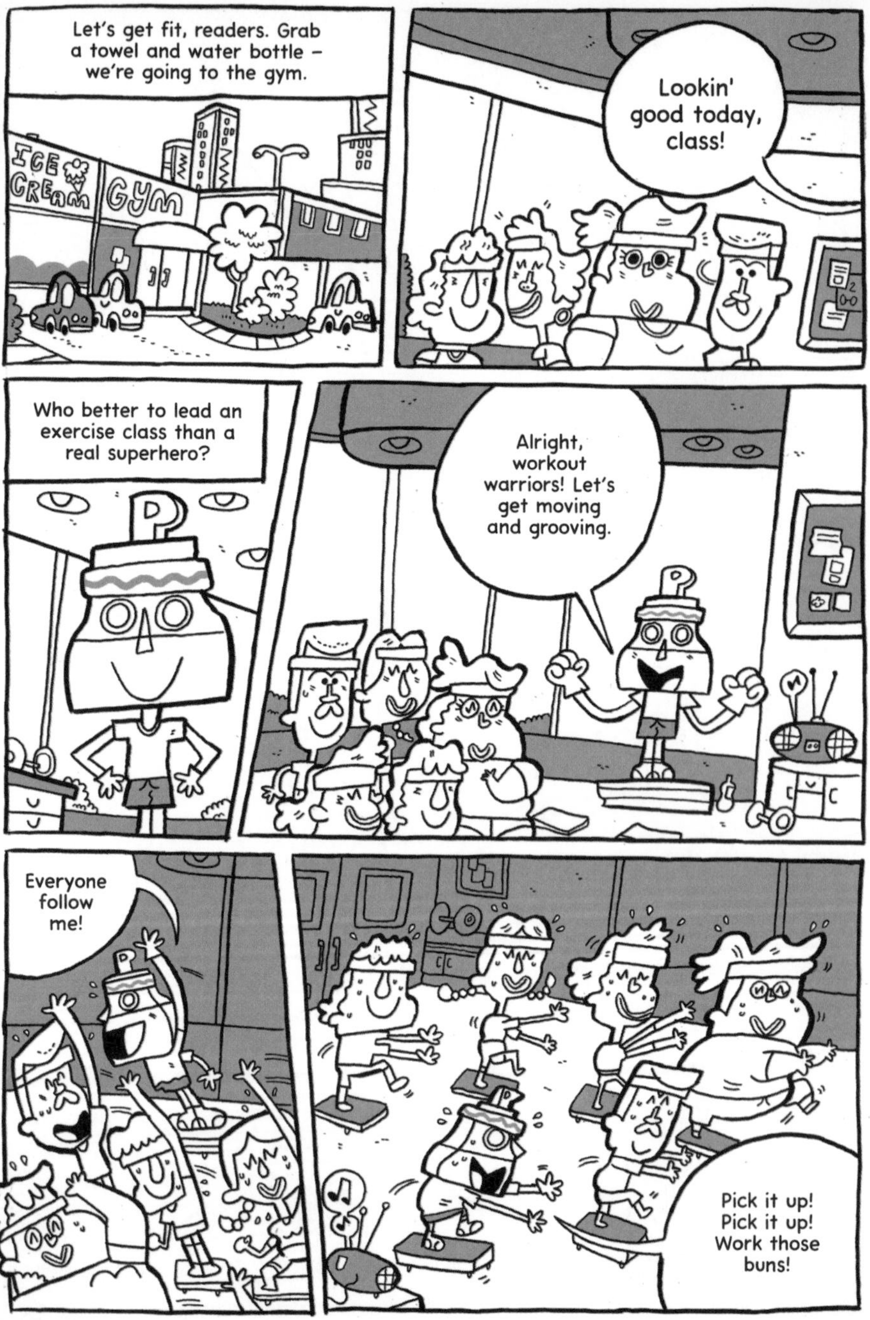
Let's get fit, readers. Grab a towel and water bottle – we're going to the gym.
ICE CREAM
GYM
Lookin' good today, class!
Who better to lead an exercise class than a real superhero?
Alright, workout warriors! Let's get moving and grooving.
Everyone follow me!
Pick it up! Pick it up! Work those buns!

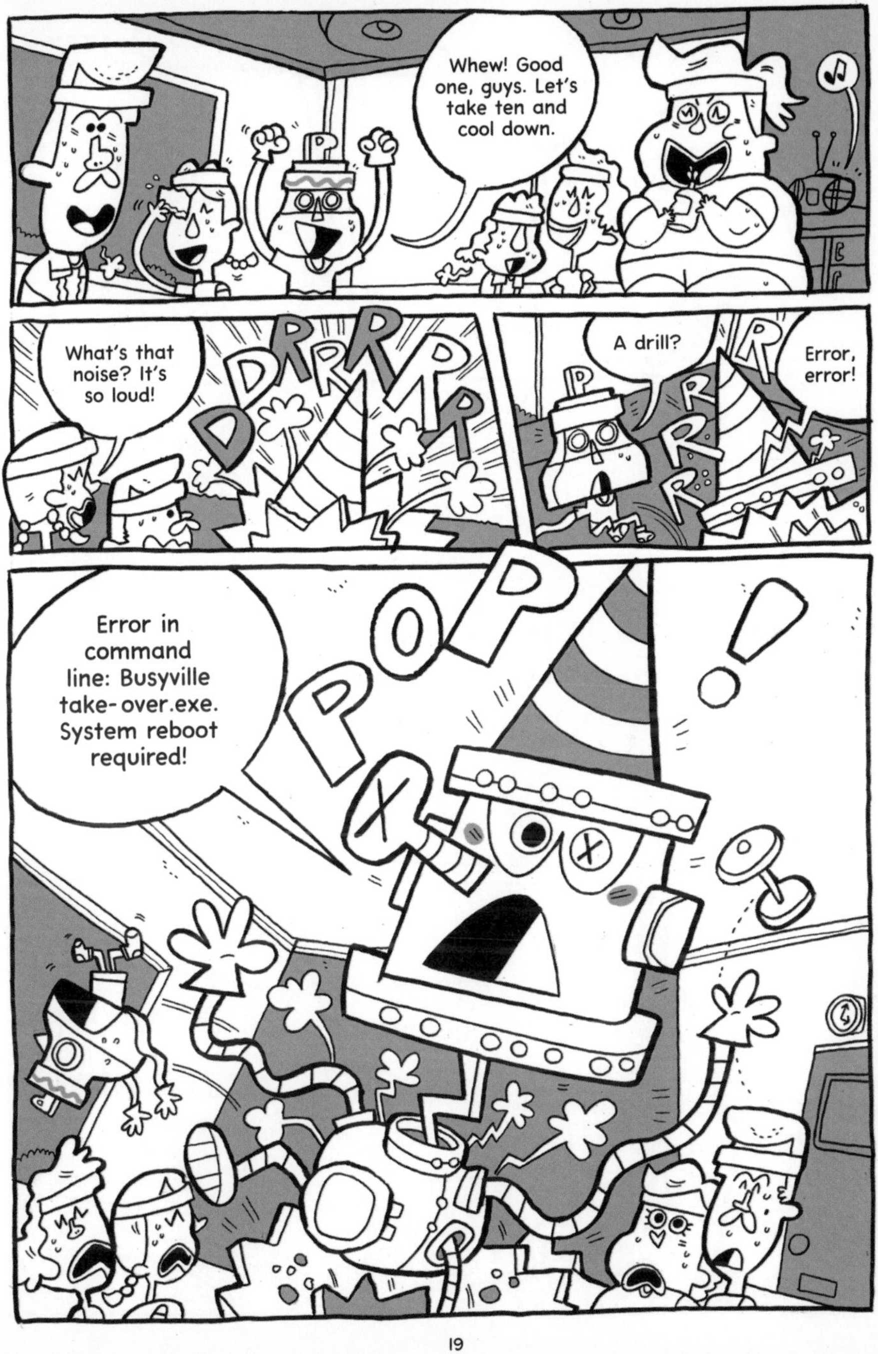
Whew! Good one, guys. Let's take ten and cool down.
What's that noise? It's so loud!
DRRRRRR
A drill?
RRRRR
Error, error!
Error in command line: Busyville take-over.exe. System reboot required!
POP!

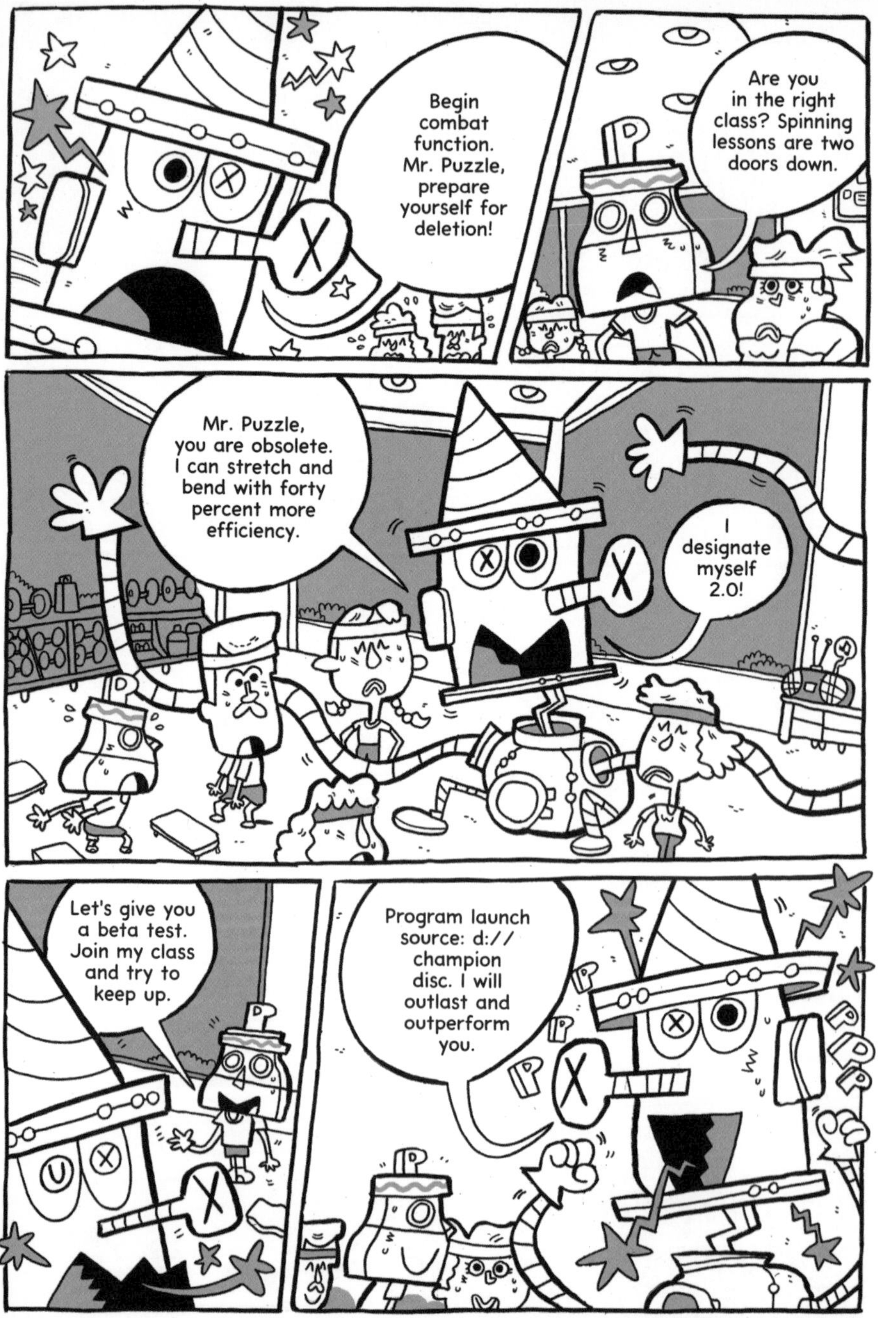
Begin combat function. Mr. Puzzle, prepare yourself for deletion!
Are you in the right class? Spinning lessons are two doors down.
Mr. Puzzle, you are obsolete. I can stretch and bend with forty percent more efficiency.
I designate myself 2.0!
Let's give you a beta test. Join my class and try to keep up.
Program launch source: d:// champion disc. I will outlast and outperform you.

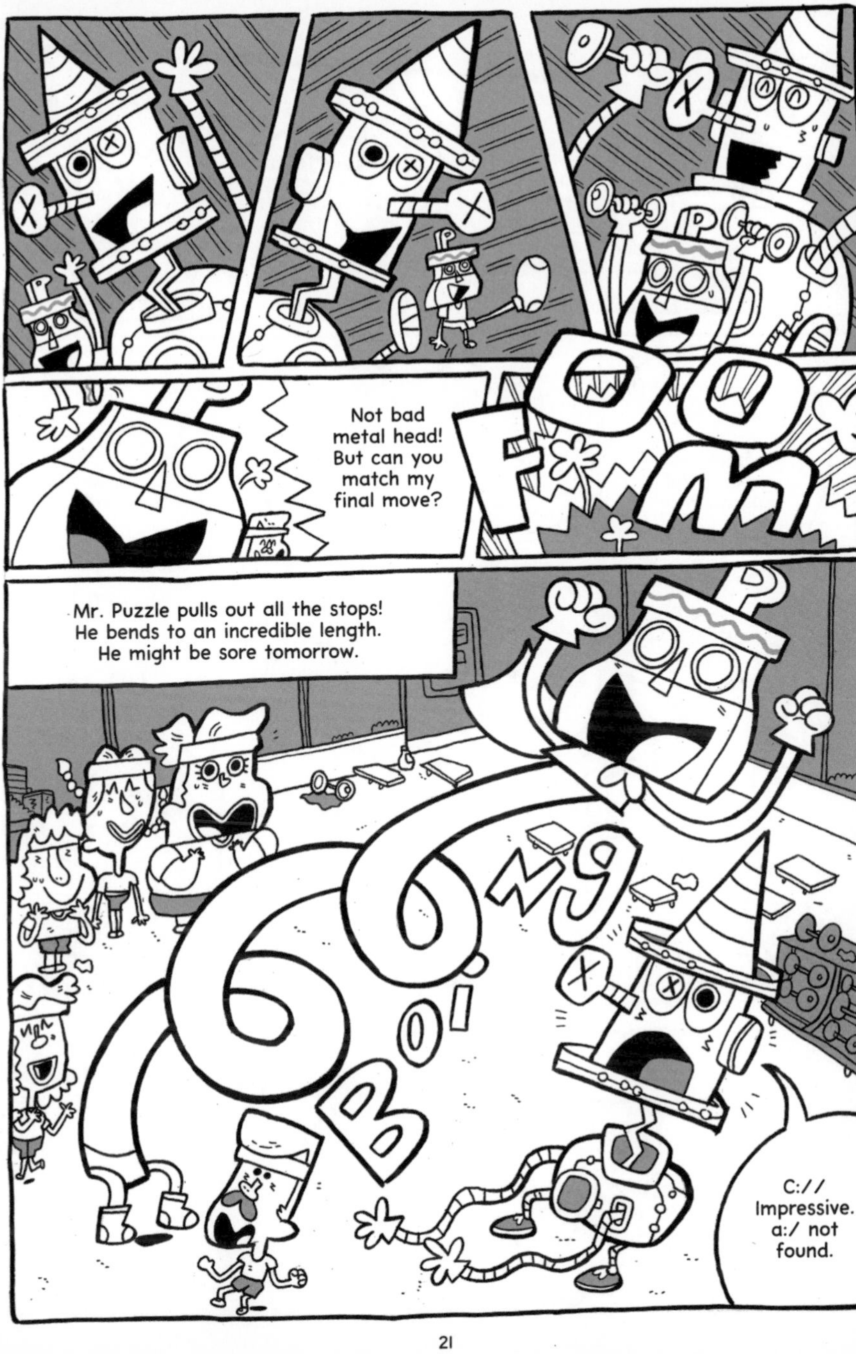
Not bad metal head! But can you match my final move?
FOOM
Mr. Puzzle pulls out all the stops! He bends to an incredible length. He might be sore tomorrow.
BOING
C:// Impressive. a:/ not found.

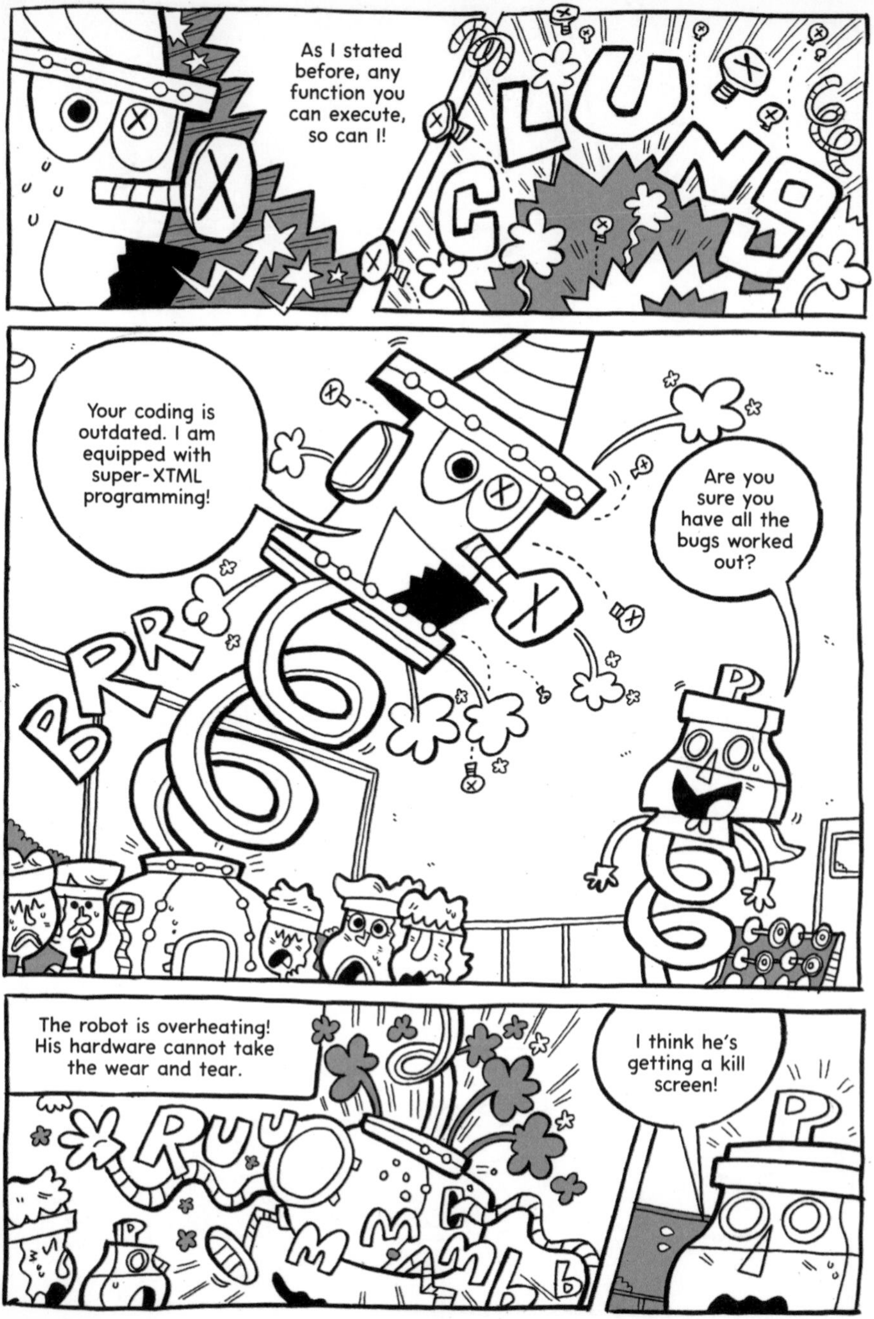
As I stated before, any function you can execute, so can I!
CLUNG
Your coding is outdated. I am equipped with super-XTML programming!
BRRR
Are you sure you have all the bugs worked out?
The robot is overheating! His hardware cannot take the wear and tear.
I think he's getting a kill screen!

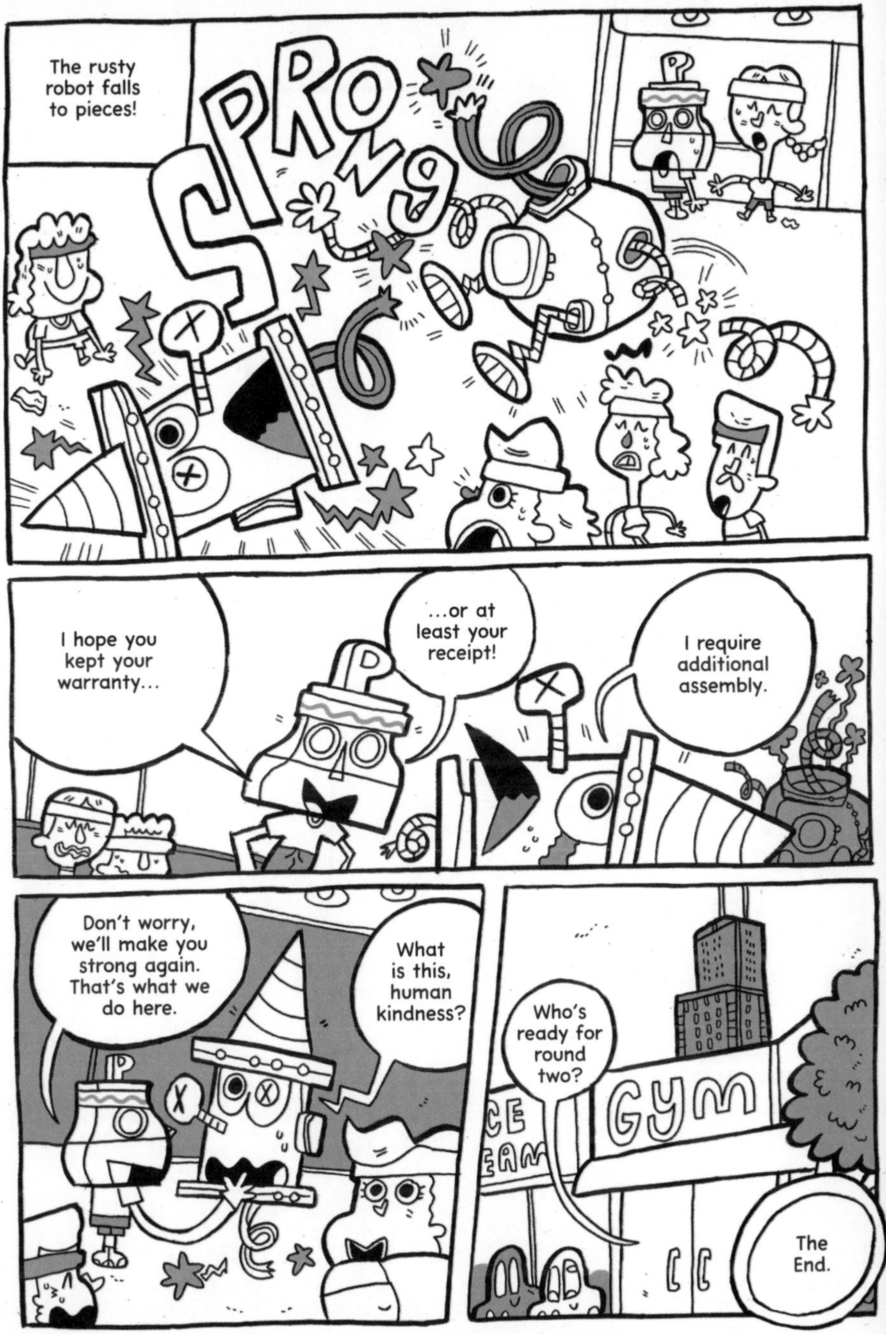
The rusty robot falls to pieces!
SPRONG
I hope you kept your warranty...
...or at least your receipt!
I require additional assembly.
Don't worry, we'll make you strong again. That's what we do here.
What is this, human kindness?
Who's ready for round two?
GYM
The End.

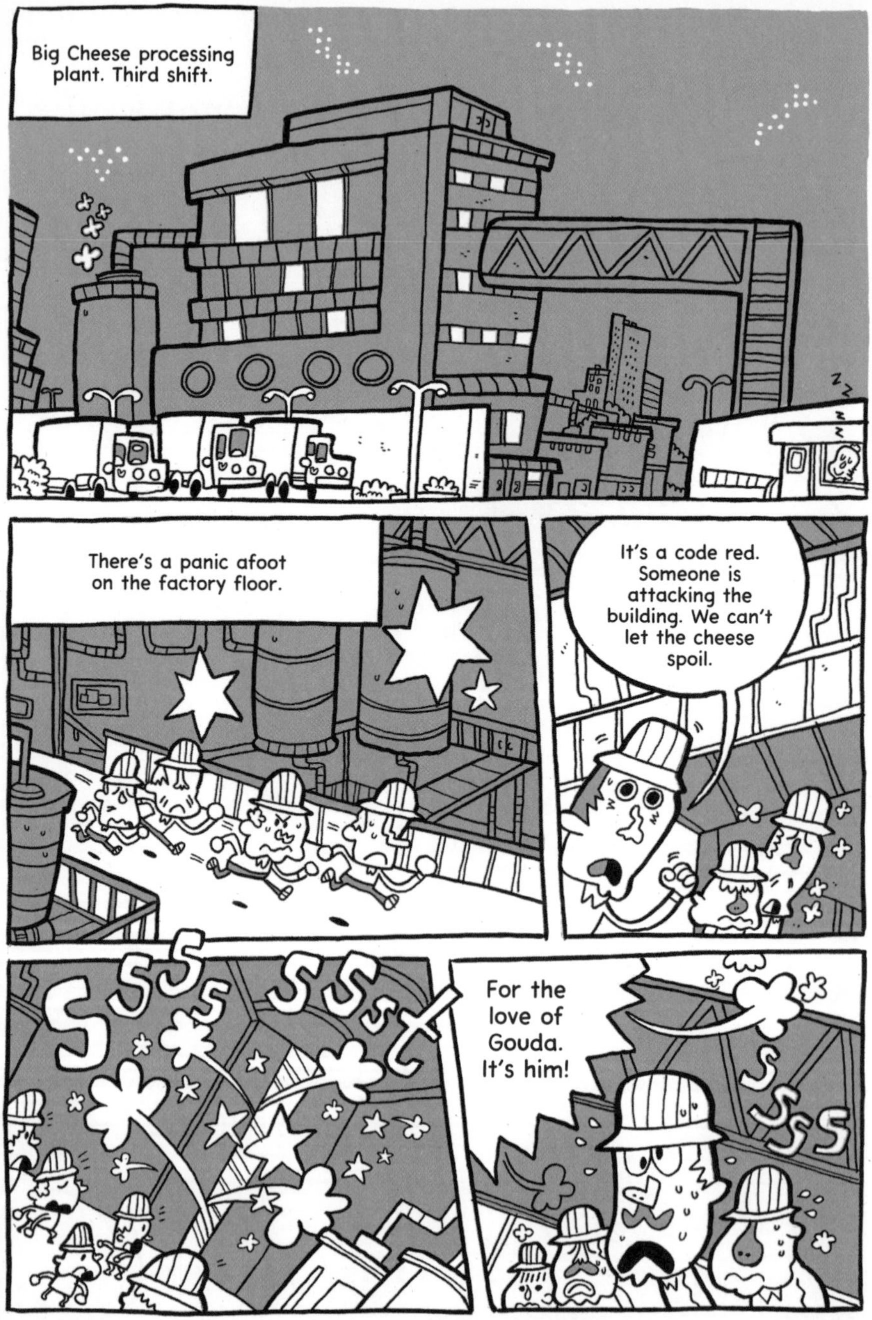

Big Cheese processing plant. Third shift.
There's a panic afoot on the factory floor.
It's a code red. Someone is attacking the building. We can't let the cheese spoil.
SSSSSSSSt
For the love of Gouda. It's him!
SSSS

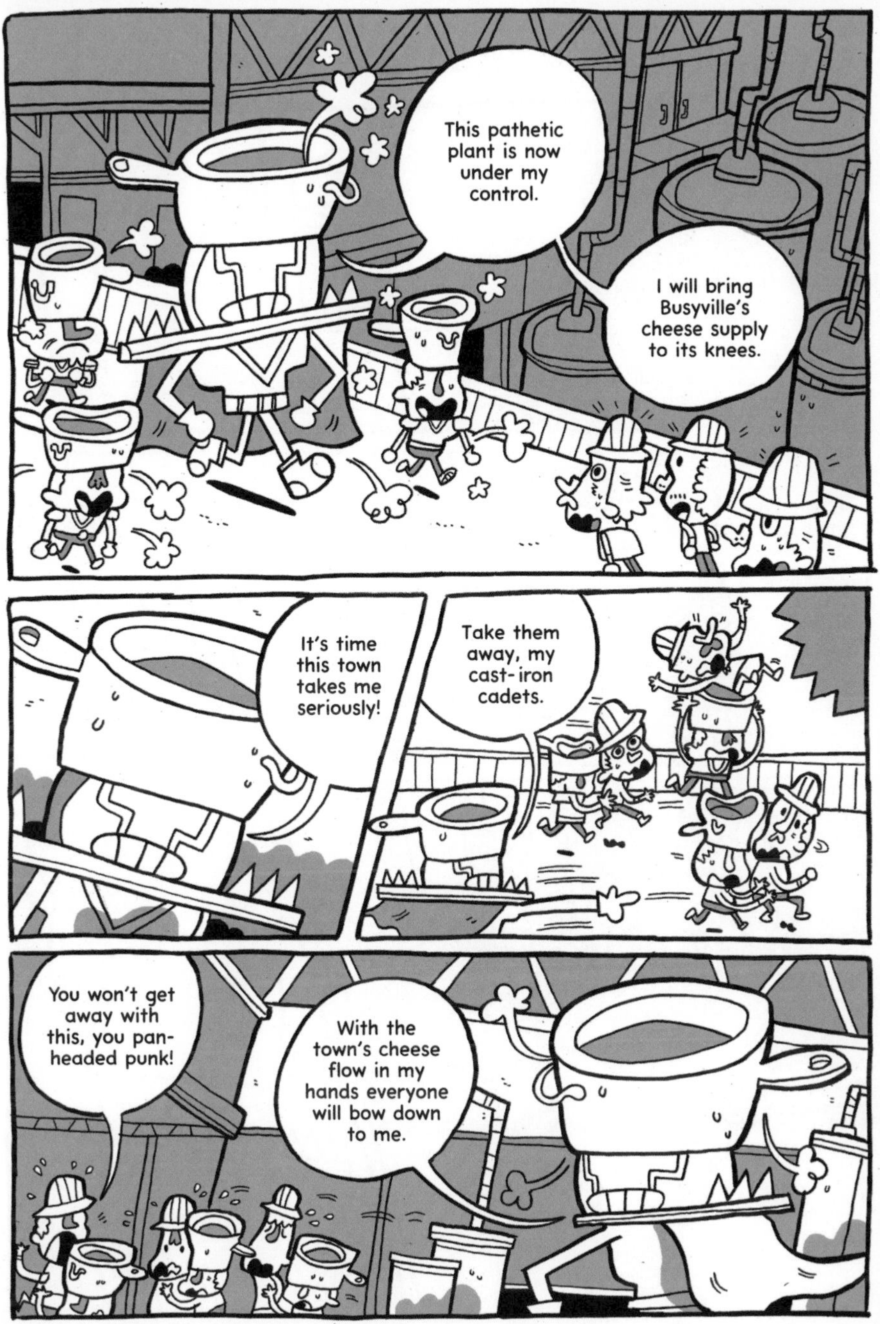
This pathetic plant is now under my control.
I will bring Busyville's cheese supply to its knees.
It's time this town takes me seriously!
Take them away, my cast-iron cadets.
You won't get away with this, you pan-headed punk!
With the town's cheese flow in my hands everyone will bow down to me.

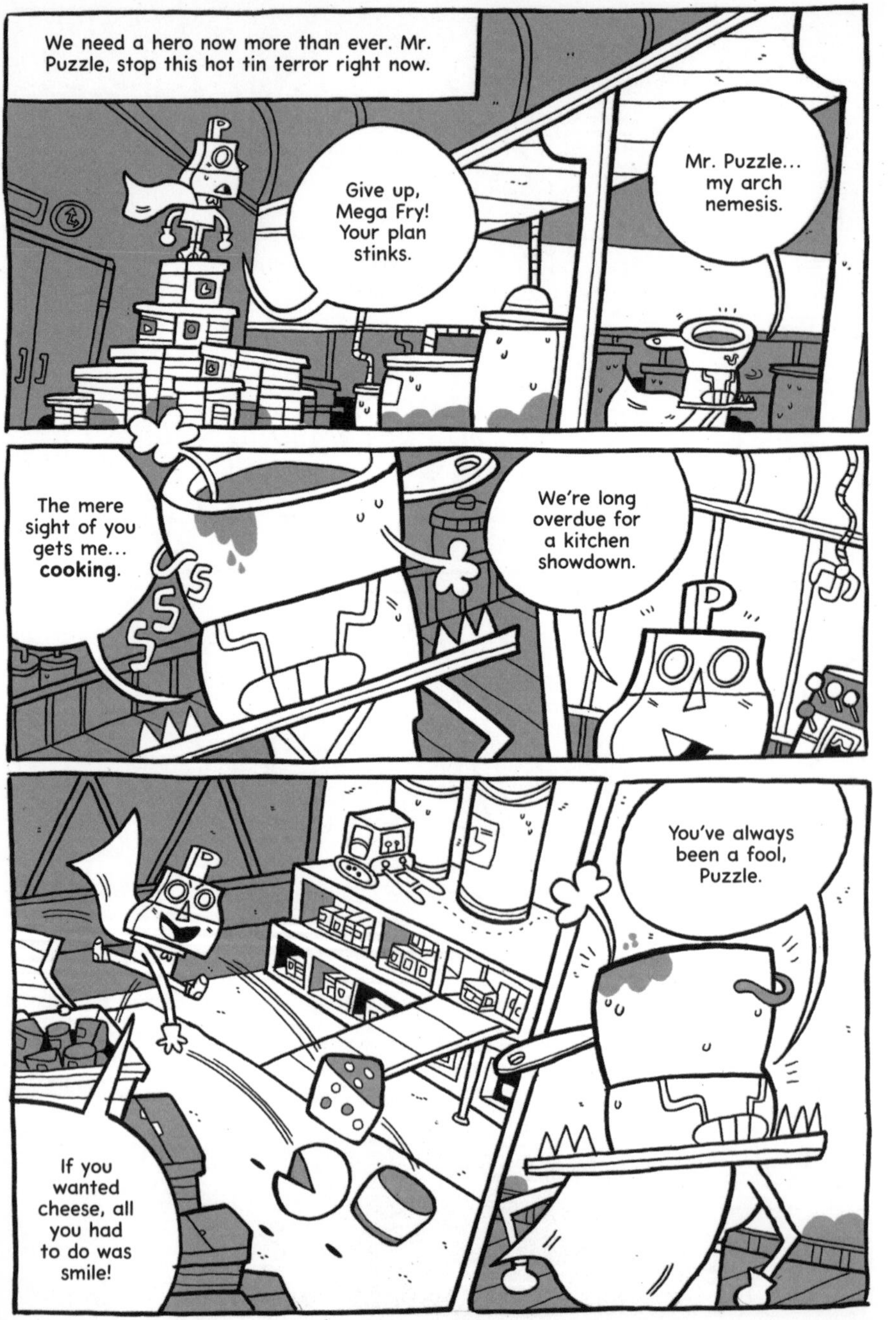
We need a hero now more than ever. Mr. Puzzle, stop this hot tin terror right now.
Give up, Mega Fry! Your plan stinks.
Mr. Puzzle... my arch nemesis.
The mere sight of you gets me... **cooking**.
We're long overdue for a kitchen showdown.
If you wanted cheese, all you had to do was smile!
You've always been a fool, Puzzle.

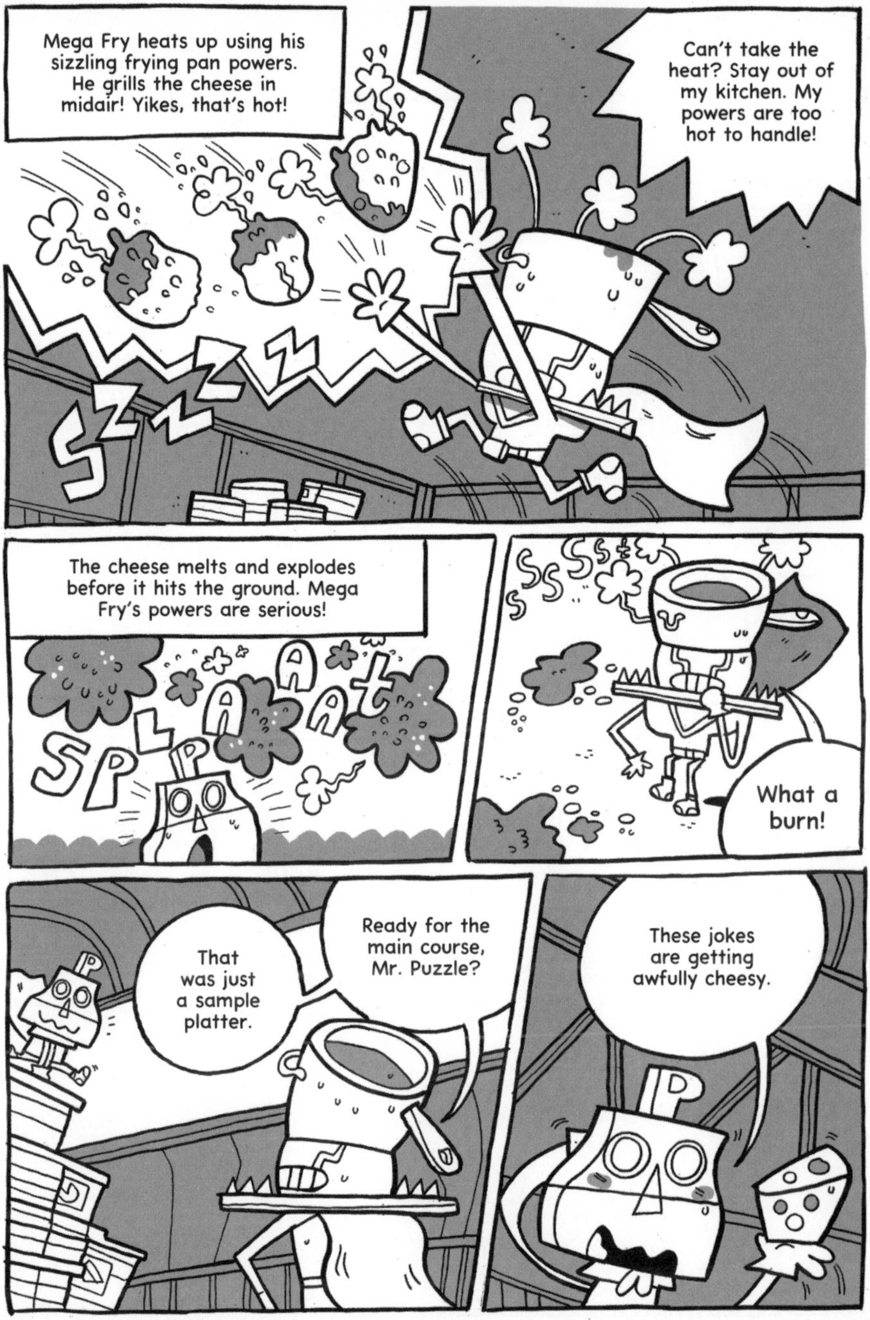
Mega Fry heats up using his sizzling frying pan powers. He grills the cheese in midair! Yikes, that's hot!
Can't take the heat? Stay out of my kitchen. My powers are too hot to handle!
The cheese melts and explodes before it hits the ground. Mega Fry's powers are serious!
SPLAAAt
What a burn!
That was just a sample platter.
Ready for the main course, Mr. Puzzle?
These jokes are getting awfully cheesy.

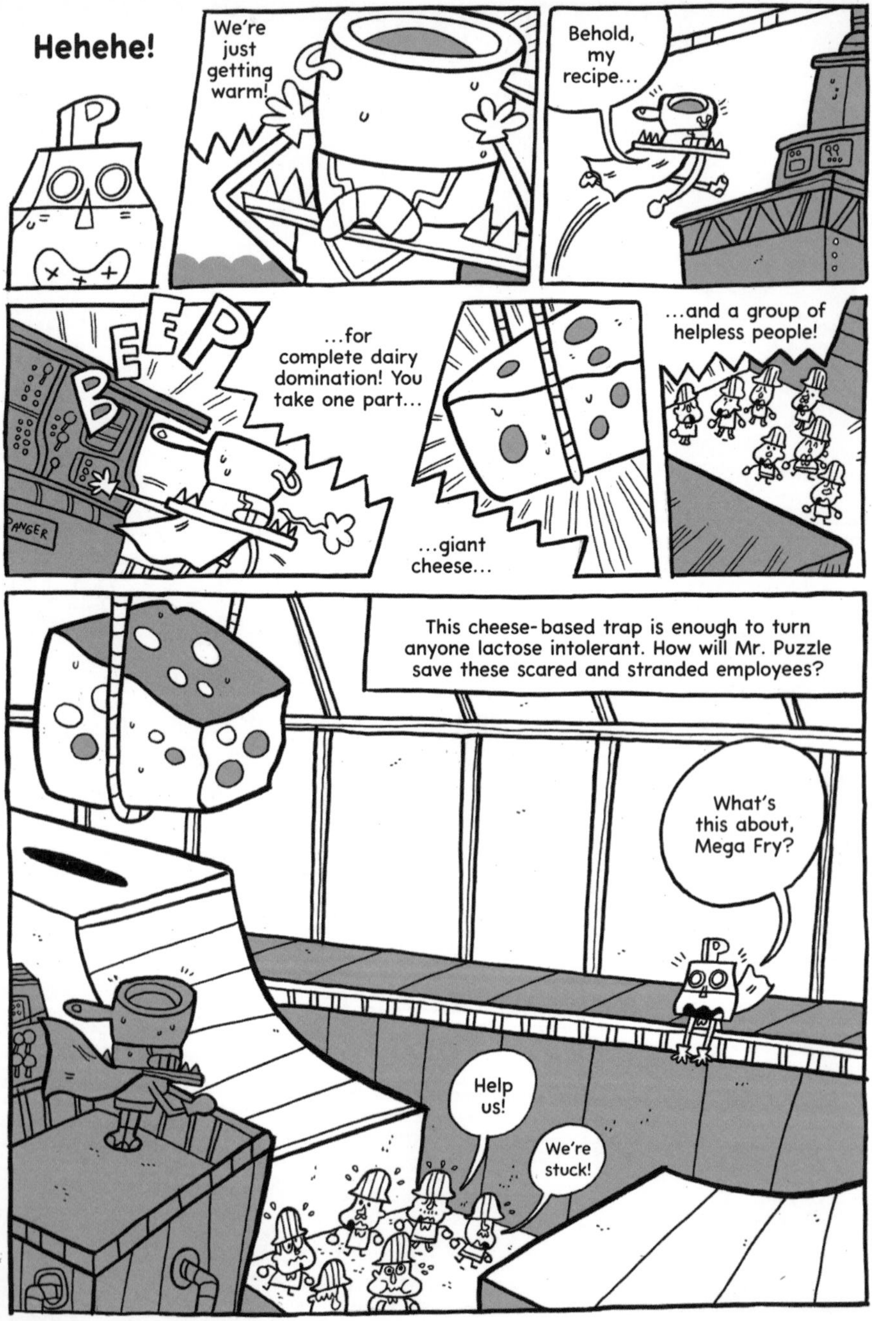
Hehehe!
We're just getting warm!
Behold, my recipe...
BEEP
...for complete dairy domination! You take one part...
...giant cheese...
...and a group of helpless people!
DANGER
This cheese-based trap is enough to turn anyone lactose intolerant. How will Mr. Puzzle save these scared and stranded employees?
What's this about, Mega Fry?
Help us!
We're stuck!

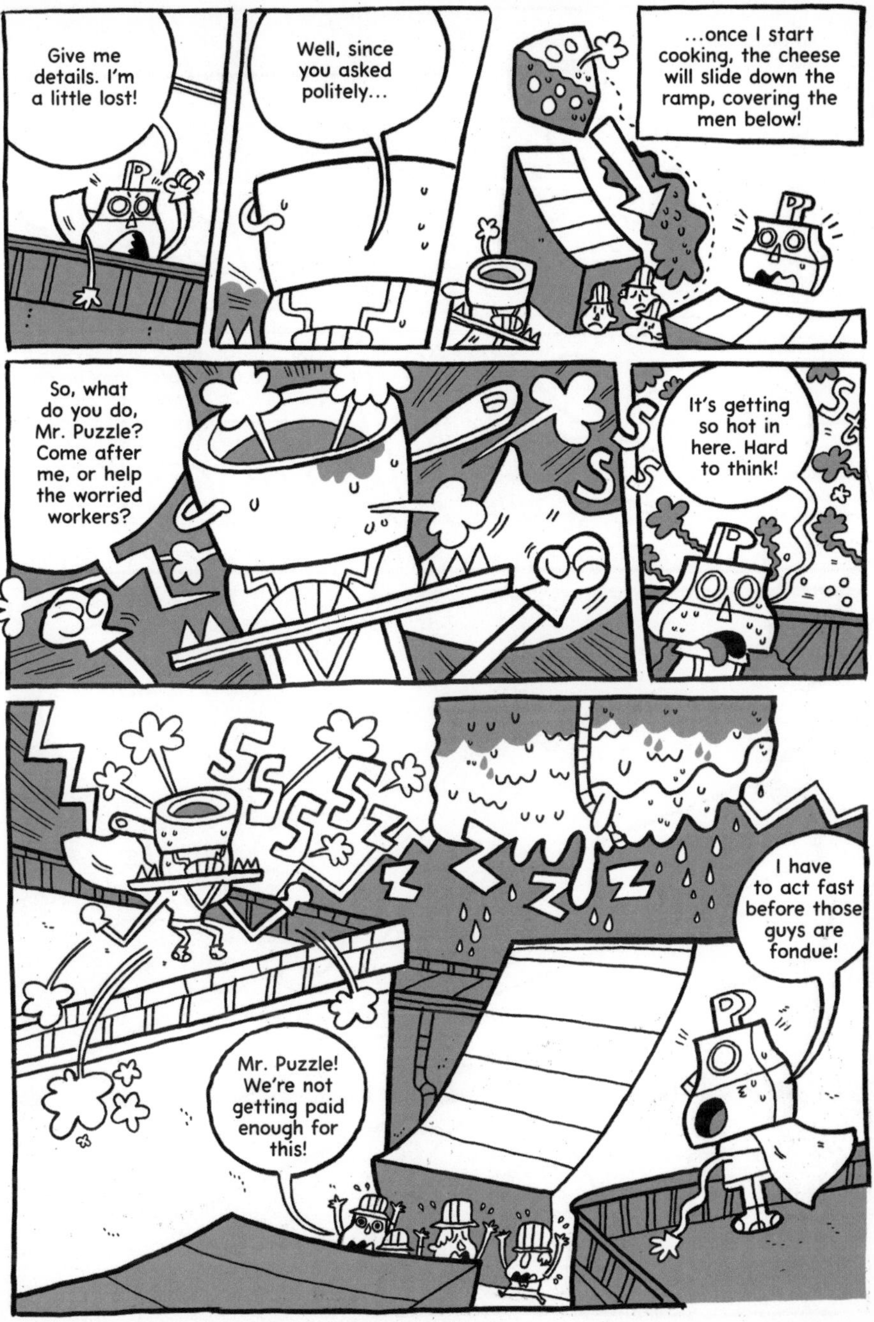

Give me details. I'm a little lost!
Well, since you asked politely...
...once I start cooking, the cheese will slide down the ramp, covering the men below!
So, what do you do, Mr. Puzzle? Come after me, or help the worried workers?
It's getting so hot in here. Hard to think!
I have to act fast before those guys are fondue!
Mr. Puzzle! We're not getting paid enough for this!

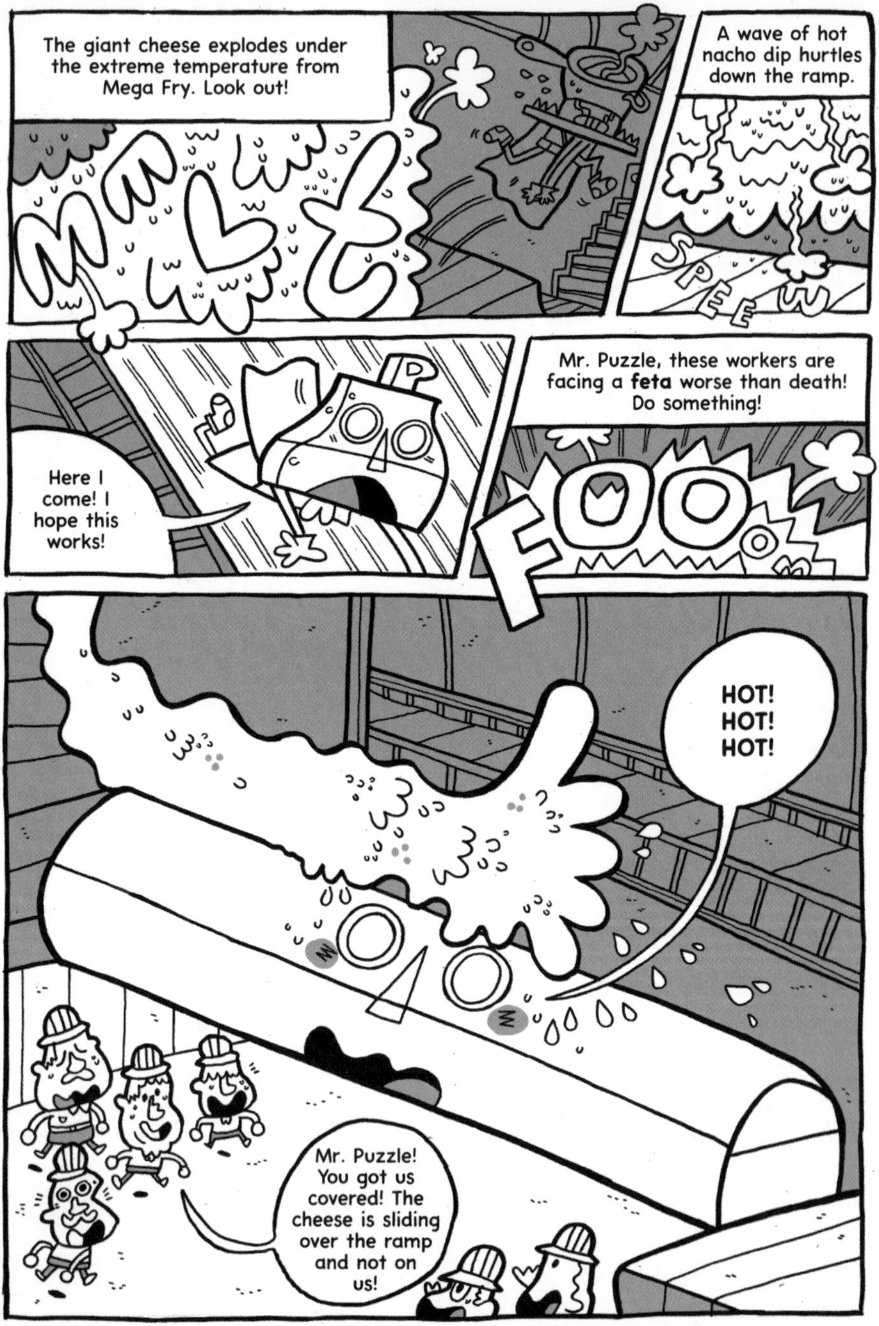
The giant cheese explodes under the extreme temperature from Mega Fry. Look out!
MELT
A wave of hot nacho dip hurtles down the ramp.
SPEEW
Here I come! I hope this works!
Mr. Puzzle, these workers are facing a **feta** worse than death! Do something!
FOOOOM
HOT! HOT! HOT!
Mr. Puzzle! You got us covered! The cheese is sliding over the ramp and not on us!

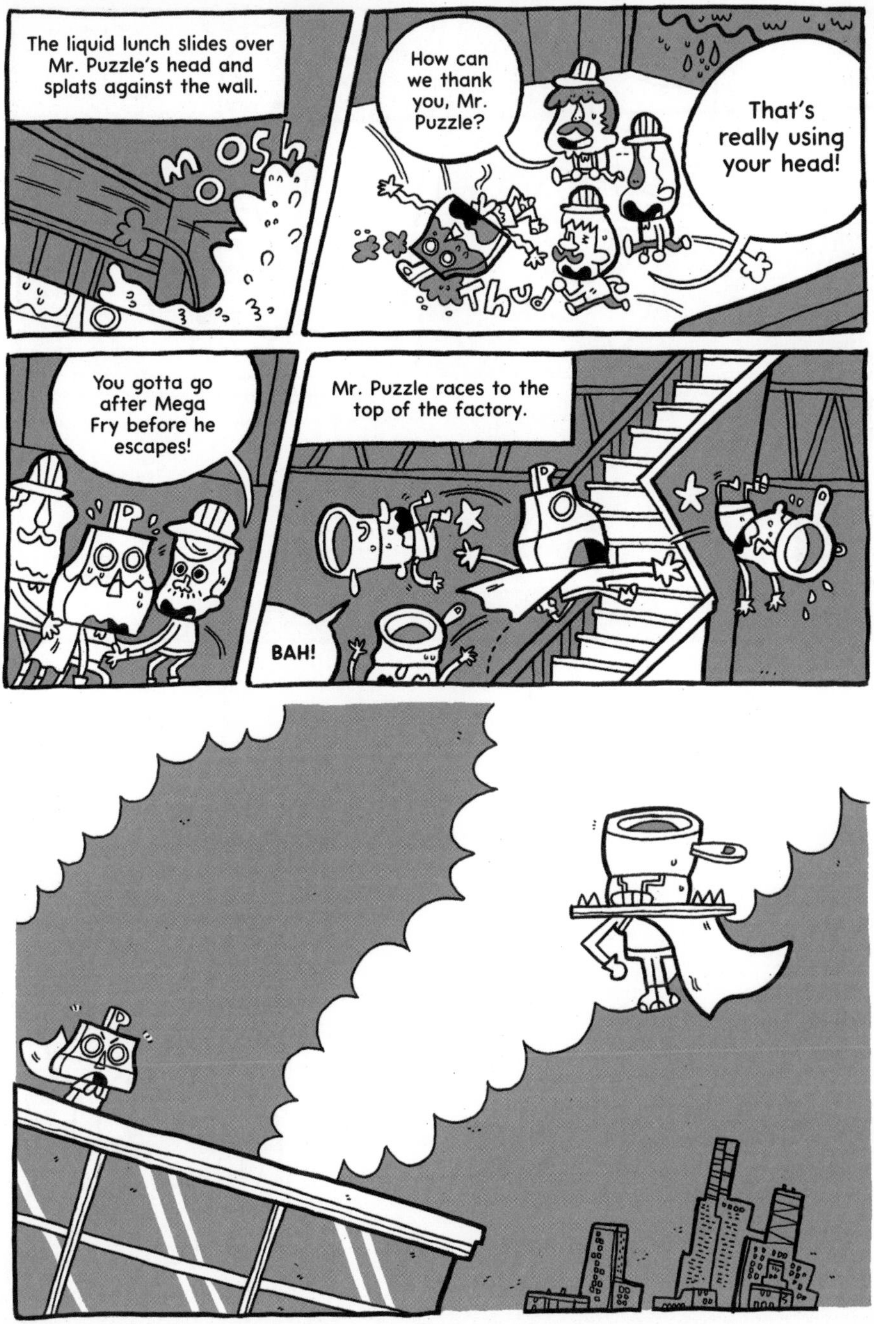
The liquid lunch slides over Mr. Puzzle's head and splats against the wall.
MOOSH
How can we thank you, Mr. Puzzle?
That's really using your head!
Thud
You gotta go after Mega Fry before he escapes!
Mr. Puzzle races to the top of the factory.
BAH!

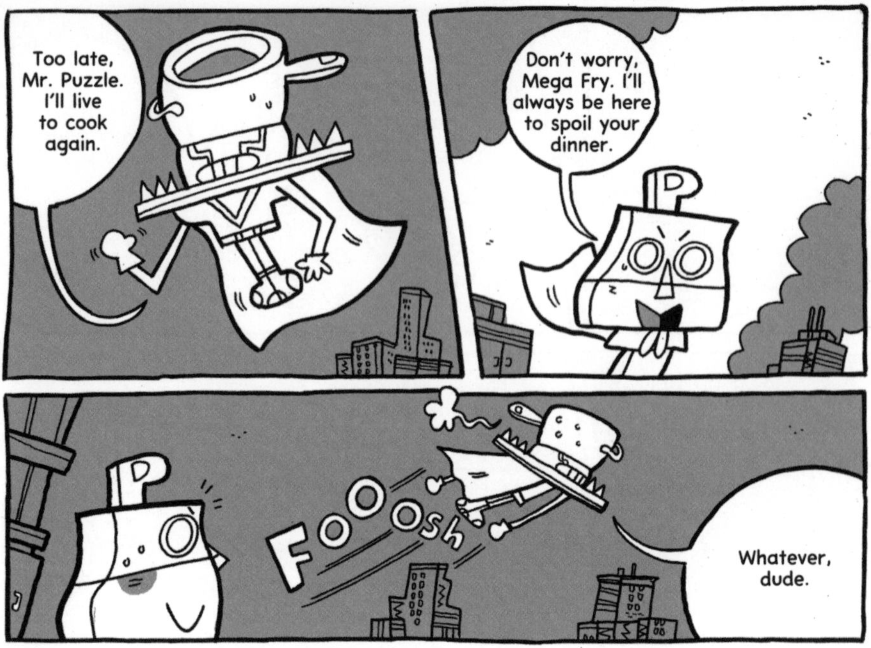
Too late, Mr. Puzzle. I'll live to cook again.
Don't worry, Mega Fry. I'll always be here to spoil your dinner.
FoOOsh
Whatever, dude.

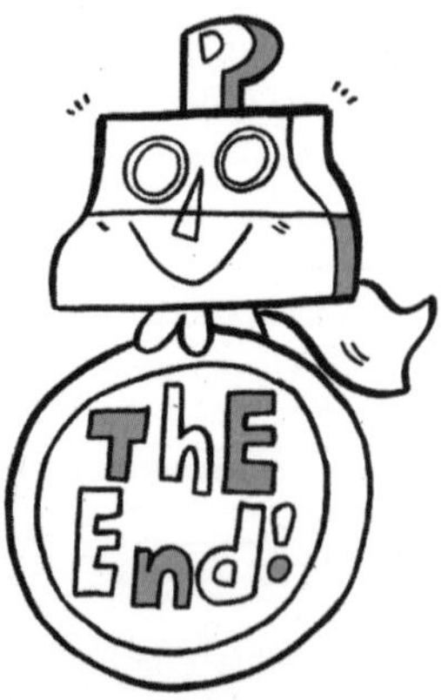
ThE End!

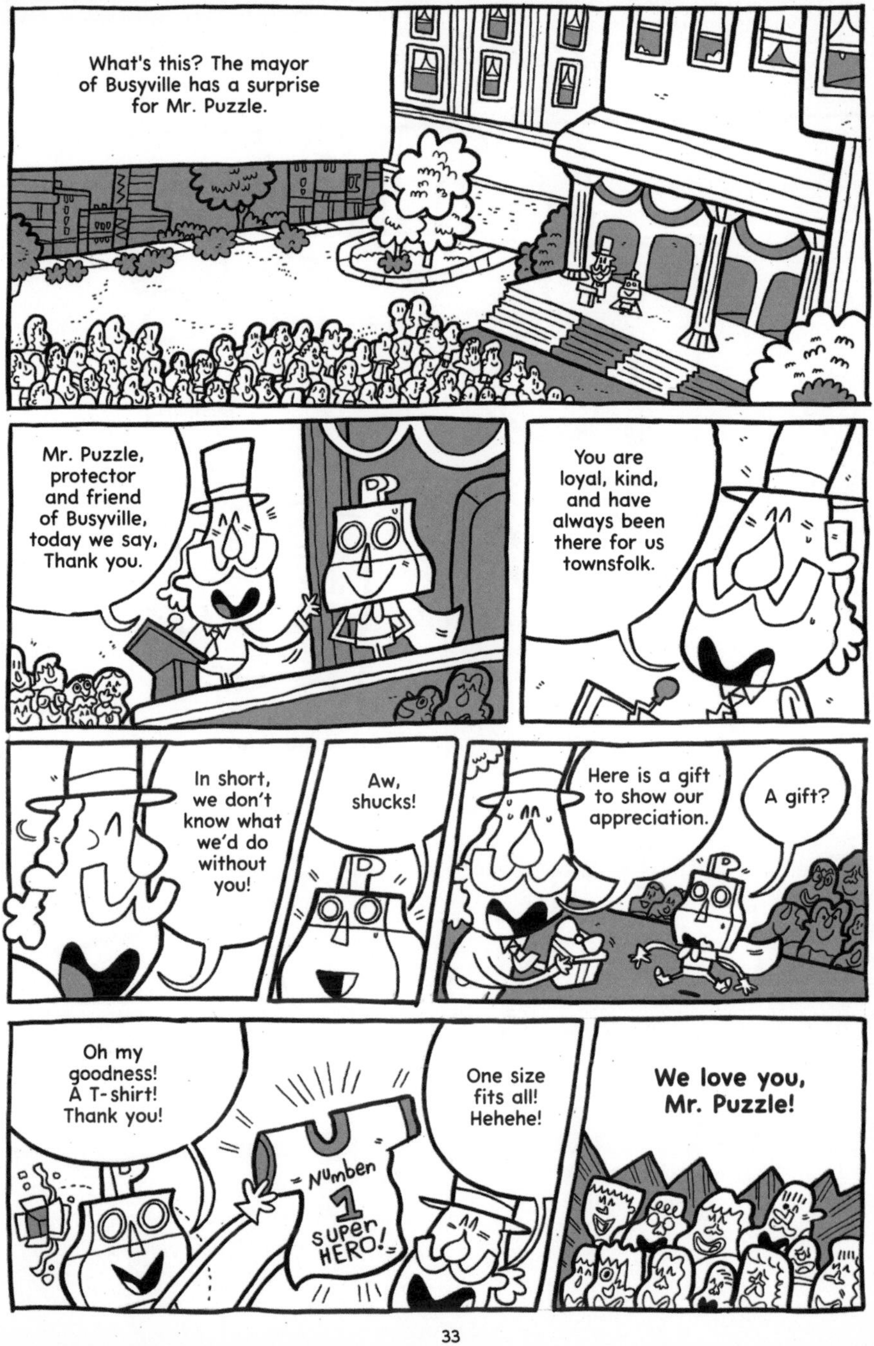
What's this? The mayor of Busyville has a surprise for Mr. Puzzle.
Mr. Puzzle, protector and friend of Busyville, today we say, Thank you.
You are loyal, kind, and have always been there for us townsfolk.
In short, we don't know what we'd do without you!
Aw, shucks!
Here is a gift to show our appreciation.
A gift?
Oh my goodness! A T-shirt! Thank you!
Number 1 SUPER HERO!
One size fits all! Hehehe!
We love you, Mr. Puzzle!

# HOW TO DRAW

MR. PUZZLE

**You'll need:**

A Pencil! 　　　　Some Paper!

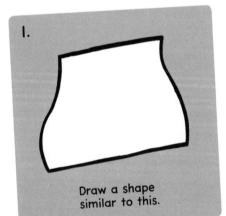

1.

Draw a shape similar to this.

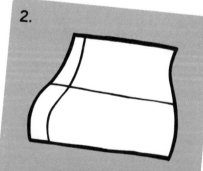

2.

Remember Mr. Puzzle needs some dimension.

**3.**

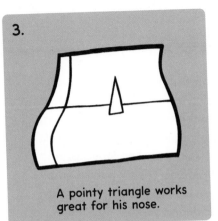

A pointy triangle works great for his nose.

**4.**

Add some circles for eyes!

**5.**

Of course he needs a mouth!

**6.**

We can't forget Mr. Puzzle's "P" and rosy cheeks!

YOU DID IT!

# CREATOR

CHRIS ELIOPOULOS is a professional illustrator and cartoonist from Chicago! He is also an adjunct professor at Columbia College Chicago in the art and design department. He is the writer and artist on several all-ages graphic novels and series: *Okie Dokie Donuts* published by Top Shelf; *Gabba Ball!* published by Oni Press; and *Monster Party* published by Koyama Press. Other clients include Disney Animation Studios, Yo Gabba Gabba!, Nick Jr., Cloudkid, and Simon and Schuster.

# Q & A

**What has been your favorite part of the book or character to tackle?**
CE: I love writing and making up bad guys. They like to shout and let everyone know why they are upset. They all act like two-year-olds with temper tantrums.

**Why should people read Mr. Puzzle?**
CE: It's a lot of fun, totally silly, and lighthearted. If this comic book were food, it would be a bag of gummy bears.

**What's your favorite part about working in comics?**
CE: Drawing all day long!

**What was the first comic you remember reading?**

CE: The Super Mario Adventures inside every issue of *Nintendo Power Magazine*.
**Tell us why everyone should read comic books!**

CE: What else are you going to read? Furniture assembly instructions or dishwasher owner manuals—yuck!

# GLOSSARY

**cadet** (kuh-DET)—a young person who is training to become a member of the armed forces

**cantankerous** (kan-TANG-kuh-ruhss)—difficult or irritating to deal with

**criticism** (KRIH-ti-siz-uhm)—a critical remark or comment

**dignity** (DIG-nuh-tee)—a quality or manner that makes a person worthy of respect

**execute** (EK-suh-kyoot)—put a plan into action

**fondue** (fawn-DOO)—a preparation of melted cheese and flavorings

**intolerant** (in-TOL-ur-uhnt)—unable or unwilling to endure

**nemesis** (NEM-uh-sis)—a formidable rival or opponent

**pathetic** (puh-THET-ik)—causing one to feel tenderness, pity, or sorrow

**phobia** (FOH-bee-uh)—an extremely strong fear

**transform** (transs-FORM)—to make a great change in something

**tussle** (TUSS-uhl)—a physical contest or struggle

**twerp** (TWERP)—a silly or unimportant person

# MR. PUZZLE
## BRAIN BENDERS!

**1.** Mr. Puzzle got his superpowers from an ancient puzzle. Imagine you are a superhero. Write a paragraph about how you gained superpowers.

**2.** Who is your favorite villain in this book – the Elephant King, Yazzo the Clown, 2.0, or Mega Fry? Explain your answer using examples from the story.

But hang on, no heat vision? Why no heat vision, Mr. Puzzle? Let me ask you this...

**3.** On page 5, the interviewer asks Mr. Puzzle why he doesn't have heat vision. What other superpowers could make Mr. Puzzle even more super?!

4. As Yazzo says on page 14, some people are afraid of clowns. List some of your worst fears, and then try to explain why these things scare you.

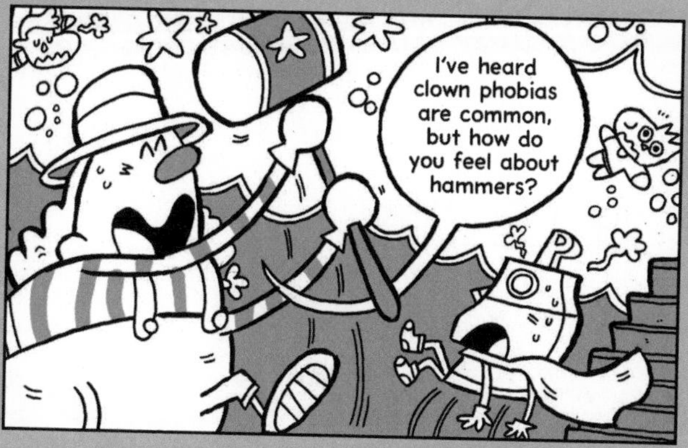
I've heard clown phobias are common, but how do you feel about hammers?

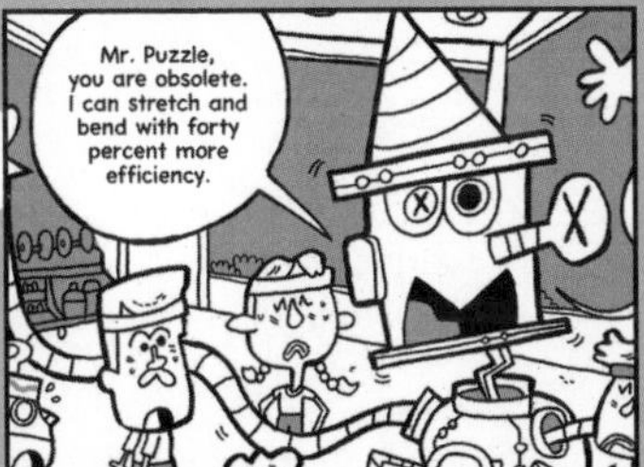
Mr. Puzzle, you are obsolete. I can stretch and bend with forty percent more efficiency.

5. The 2.0 robot wanted to be a better, more advanced version of Mr. Puzzle. Do you think the robot succeeded? Why or why not?

6. At the end of this comic, Mr. Puzzle was awarded a T-shirt for his good deeds. How would you reward Mr. Puzzle for saving the day, time and time again?

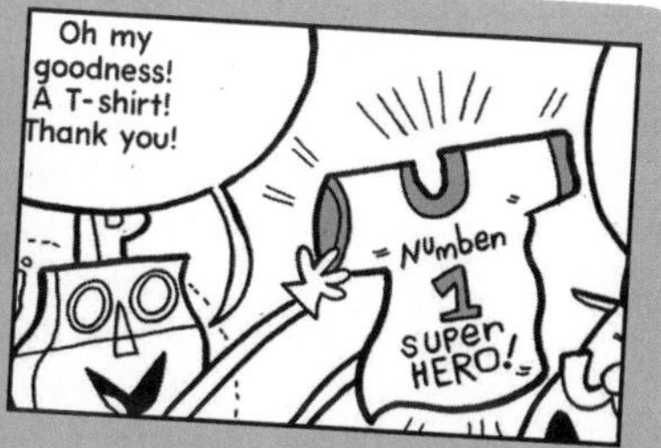
Oh my goodness! A T-shirt! Thank you!
Number 1 SUPER HERO!

The **Mr. PUZZLE** fun doesn't
stop here! Discover more at...

# WWW.CAPSTONEKIDS.com

Find cool websites and more books
like this one at **www.facthound.com**

Just type in the Book ID:
**9781434260260**
And you're ready to go!